Galaxy Revisited

By Harlowe Frost

ISBN eBook: 978-1-959981-75-6
ISBN paperback: 978-1-959981-76-3

Editor: Weslee Imrisek
Developmental Editor: Elizabeth Daly
Developmental Editor: Dulaine Roode
Cover Art: Getcovers.com
Formatting: Huckleberry Rahr

Acknowledgements

I've really enjoyed stretching my creativity into space. Some time ago I was on a reader page where someone asked for a book similar to a series that combined fantasy and sci-fi. I loved the other series and decided I wanted that ... and sapphic to boot!

As always, I follow the lead of my characters. There's a little planning, but most of what I do is write incident reports. Enjoying the stories as they unfold.

I'll admit my oldest child loves this series. He doesn't read them fully, he isn't into spice, but he loves everything else. He helps me brainstorm and figure out the ins and outs of what's going on. This may be one of the only series he pushed more than I did!

As for the other people who helped this series come to life, as always, Wes Imrisek, is the best editor. I am blessed to have someone so amazing in my life. I also want to that Elizabeth Daly and Dulaine Roode for always being willing to read my words.

Beyond everything, the readers. I love telling stories and it tickles me that there are people out there who enjoy reading them!

You Teach Me? I Teach You!

Betsy

Betsy gave Viera a hug, rubbing her back.
"Are you patting me down? Worried I'm taking something with me?" Her friend laughed as she pulled away, her eyes moist with unshed tears.

The two moved apart, but their hands clasped. "Of course, I am. You ate a pound of sugars. I don't know if you're trustworthy."

From the other side of the kitchen, Violet snorted. "I wouldn't pat you down. I'd question the choice of food you're bringing. Why not take sushi? It's so good here!"

Both Betsy and Viera turned to her. Betsy's eyebrow rose and she couldn't stop the chuckle. "Really? Raw fish? How long do you think it would last?"

Violet slumped. "Yeah, if you're going to be logical, I guess. But it's just ... sushi!"

With a shake of her head, Viera gave each of them one more hug. "I'm going to miss both of you. It's been nice being home again, but it's time." She headed over to the panel and dialed up the Ziner. Moments later she was gone, and this time Betsy didn't think she'd be seeing her friend again for a long time. Viera had a new life with Thorn on Abritos, and galivanting throughout the galaxy wasn't part of the bargain.

Gazing off into space, Betsy thought about the years she'd known the other woman. Viera had changed so much from the introverted second grade teacher she'd first met. It amazed her that one spring break had taken her friend, given her magic, and brought her the love of her life. The fact that it led her to a new planet made her a bit sad, but now that Viera was a wizard, they both had years to meet up and grow together.

It amazed her that she had ever befriended a regular human in the first place. Despite how busy Betsy was in her day-to-day job, she always tried to get out and relax. Years—centuries—on the job had taught her that. She'd been walking around one of Madison's lakes when she first saw Viera. There were so many people, the other woman hadn't registered on her radar, until the two had walked the same path, practically together, every day for a week.

At the end of the week, Viera had come up to Betsy, smiling wide. "Hi, I'm Viera. I don't know if you've noticed, but we seem to be walking together. I figure we may as well talk while we walk. I'm new to town and would love someone to help distract me from the beautiful scenery."

Betsy laughed and decided a new friend sounded great. Over the years, she'd been very selective on which short-lived humans she'd allowed into her life, but the spunk and dry humor convinced Betsy to give Viera a chance.

When Thorn, the Commander of the chanzii, whose planet had been invaded, needed a place with a good elementary school, she knew exactly which one to suggest. She hadn't expected the two to connect as well as they had, but in reality, she wasn't upset about it.

I'm really glad Viera has finally found someone ... and traveled more than a few miles from Madison. It's good for her.

Arms wrapped around Betsy's waist. "Hey, where did you go?" Violet's voice soothed her, and Betsy leaned back, sinking into the embrace.

Just like Viera found Thorn from the refugees from Abritos, Betsy found Violet ... or maybe it was the other way around. Either way, Betsy's life was improving every day with the inclusion of the other woman.

"I was just remembering how I met Viera and thinking about how much her life has changed." Betsy swiveled so she faced the beautiful alien. She gave Violet a soft kiss, enjoying that she had the option to do that action with the lovely alien. "Now, are you still hungry or should we discuss the rest of the day?"

Violet's arms tightened. "It's still early, can the day stay here?" Her body shimmied against Betsy.

A moan escaped Betsy as her hands skimmed up to tangle in Violet's silky hair. After enjoying a deeper kiss, she sighed. "I promised Devlin I'd come to his first lesson on gem magic today. If I hadn't, I'd let you decide all our activities for the weekend."

"Hmm," Violet hummed. "As long as that option is available in the future, I'm okay with waiting." Her eyes narrowed. "I can think of a few ways to keep you tied up ... er, busy during a weekend."

Betsy wasn't sure the first statement was really a slip of the tongue. From the start, Violet had proven herself dominant.

Before she could respond, Violet scrunched up her nose and asked, "But what will I do while you're learning magic? Should I join you in Africa or head home?"

"Why not try out the lesson?" Betsy shrugged, curiosity filling her. "You never know. I hear Devlin is an excellent teacher."

The land around them shifted from the bright early afternoon Wisconsin woods to the early evening manicured campus around the school. Though Betsy usually left the ven, her large moth-like pets, at home, everyone here knew about aliens, and she thought the trip would be fun for them.

As soon as they landed, Wes, black as a shadow, darted off to explore. There were squeals and gasps from the far side of the school building.

"What is that ... is it dangerous? Poisonous? Are we in danger?" Betsy thought she recognized Dulce's voice, a woman from Colorado who they recently found with magic.

Though Wes had flown off like a shot, Buttercup, less rambunctious, but just as sociable, followed at a more sedate pace. Her gray fur with the black markings looked haughty in the way she circled around the corner.

Peals of laughter followed the exclamation. "Mom, look at them. The black one landed on

Devlin's shoulder ... and is it purring?" *That must be Trinity, Dulce's daughter.*

Betsy and Violet had reached the side of the school and saw everyone else. Buttercup circled just above the group. Kafi watched for them, a wide smile on his face. Next to him was Devlin, who had reached up to scratch Wes, the attention whore who'd landed on his shoulder. All the students from the school sat on benches, gaping at the creatures.

Kafi chuckled. "Well, that's one way to enter, my friend. I didn't know you were bringing the ven." He looked up. "Buttercup, are you going to find someone to pet you or do you want to explore?"

After another few lazy beats of her wings, Buttercup dropped down and landed by Trinity on the table near her hand. The teen's face lit up as she started to scratch and pet with enthusiasm.

Satisfied that the ven were settled, Betsy and Violet sat at a table. Then Betsy smiled at the people she knew. "Hi, everyone. These two are Westley and Buttercup. They are ven, brother and sister, and very friendly. As you can see, they just like attention ... that is, until they decide they want to go and fly around."

Devlin huffed out a laugh. "Okay, now that we've gotten the last of our students—"

"Not the last, youngling," Balzeno's gruff voice interrupted him. The dwarf came over to sit next to Betsy. "A new magic system? I haven't learned something new in ... well, in a millennia of your Earth years? Maybe. I honestly haven't tried to figure out this conversion, but we can all agree it's been a long time. Something different intrigues me."

The air in the courtyard where they sat seemed to still as everyone contemplated his words. Betsy knew he was ancient, but that would put him probably over two thousand years old. It hurt her head to imagine everything he'd seen.

She chuckled. "Okay, grandpa, let's see if the young bucks can teach us old dogs any new tricks."

Her words seemed to break everyone from their stupor, and they all turned back to Devlin. He snapped his slack jaw shut then slowly smiled. "Okay, let's learn about imbuing items. My town imbues an array of items: tinctures, soaps and shampoos, food, paper, gems ... Over the years, centuries even, our ancestors found all sorts of things that they could push their magic into."

Jerome raised his hand. He was the last of the Colorado family. Though more and more people were arriving with magic around the world, it didn't always show up in full families like this one. "When you say, 'push their magic,' are you talking about the same thing we've been learning about? I thought that this was something different."

A woman in the back with ash-blond hair and blue eyes raised her hand. It took Betsy a moment to remember her name. Devlin smiled at her. "Soleil, do you want to add to his question or answer it?"

That's it, one of the Oz residents who also has wizard magic. They came to help teach their brand of magic as well as learn ours.

"I was hoping to answer it." Everyone rotated to look at her, and she smiled. "What we're learning here from Kafi and the other Pillars is how to reach into ourselves and control this well within us. It's this power that's amazing. What we do in Oz is different. We work with the world around us, in harmony. I always imagined we asked the Mother Earth to give of herself to allow us to have this amazing thing. I know now that the magic is more in the air than the land, but the idea of the Earth giving to us just makes me happy."

Up front, Devlin nodded. "I agree. What we do isn't an internal magic, it's more of a request answered." He held up two jade stones. "We use these to create communication gems. I know you all use cell phones, but our type of magic, pulling power from the ether, messes with technology. Oh! If you have a cell phone on you, turn it off if you don't want to have to replace it."

All around the courtyard, Betsy saw people pull out their phones and fiddle with them. Betsy and Violet did the same.

Next to her, Balzeno narrowed his eyes. "Why haven't you created some sort of gem, or leather pouch that protects your phone from the magic?"

Devlin opened his mouth, then snapped it shut. "I don't know, that is an excellent question. I'll have to work on that next."

Everyone laughed.

"Okay," Devlin continued, once he saw the phones all put away. "We're going to create a pair of communication stones. The idea behind this is that if two people have a pair with matching symbols, they should be able to communicate. In Oz, we create a bunch with the same symbol and it's about the person focusing on who they want to speak with, that way we don't have to carry a bunch of stones. But that is a bit more complicated. We'll start with a single stone-to-stone walkie-talkie imbue."

Kafi walked around and handed two jade stones out to each person. Once he got back to the front, he took two for himself, then went to sit at the table with Betsy and crew.

Devlin nodded. "Okay, there are a few ways we imbue. We can do the traditional cauldron that you've seen many witches use, but that's mostly for tinctures, soaps, and foods. It's also used for part of the process to make paper. Most of our imbuing involves an aspect of chanting. I think a lot of the chanting is to focus our will. The last thing we do are pictograms."

"Like runes?" Trinity asked, the suddenness of her question shocked Buttercup, and the ven took to the air. Wes followed and the two were off to explore.

"Not really. I mean, you could if you're an expert on runes, but we do small pictures to show what we want. You could write words, and sometimes witches do on the paper for their magic, but full words on a gem is ... complicated, and obnoxious."

Trinity's nose scrunched up. "Oh, yeah, I can see that." She focused on one of the jade stones, turning it in her hand. "I can't imagine writing on this."

Laughter followed her words.

Once everyone had a moment to think about engraving the stones, Devlin said, "What we're going to do is create a set of circles in the dirt. The first should be large enough that you, as an individual, can sit in it and it will contain your work. You will create two smaller circles, one within the circle you'll be sitting in, one outside, about a foot from your larger working space. Within these two smaller circles, you'll place the two jade stones. I have imbued rope—created from braided boiled yarn, horse tail, and candlestick wick—that you can use to connect the two smaller circles.

"You'll chant, like we learned this morning, while you create your setup, to make it more than just drawings in the dirt. When you engrave the jade with an oval, to represent a mouth, and something uniquely your own, if you did everything correctly, both stones should get the etching at the same time. The better the link, the better the symmetry."

Sounds of amazement came from the group. Betsy agreed. The idea of what he said amazed her.

Devlin answered a few questions and went over the steps one more time, reminding everyone about the words of the chant. Then they headed out to the back field to try their hand at imbuing.

A Tall Tale

Betsy

The jade stone Betsy held fit in the palm of her hand. Etching a circle in the dirt and then two parallel squiggly lines to the right, she focused, trying to let the ambient magic around her flow through her hands to the gem. She chanted the words Devlin had taught the class, softly, over and over, letting them carry the magic and her intent.

The idea of this magic excited her. It had been a long time since she'd done anything so new or foreign.

When she finished, she sat back and let her muscles relax. Then, she picked up the other gem and rubbed her thumb over the spot that had the matching etching. "Thank the gods," she mumbled low. Part of her worried she'd fail completely. It wasn't her style of magic, but she felt she should be at least a bit proficient.

Around the field, other people still worked. As she manipulated her spell, she hadn't focused on anyone else, but it surprised her to see Violet standing near Devlin, smiling wide, hands animated as the two spoke. Their voices were low, but they were deep in discussion.

Betsy pushed herself to her feet and saw Balzeno doing the same. She walked over to him. "What do you think, Elder?"

"None of that, or I'll start calling you Elder as well, Pillar Doeth. How about while here, you call me Balzeno, as my friends do, and I'll call you—" one of his bushy brows lifted.

Chuckling softly, Betsy nodded. "Betsy. That would be best."

"Perfect," he said with a smirk. "Now, let's go speak with the young expert and see how we did."

When they reached Violet and Devlin, Violet spun to Betsy with a grin. "Did you love it? I loved doing it. It felt so natural. Did your twin gems work?" The chanzii major bounced by the end of her questions.

Betsy found herself smiling wide at Violet's exuberance. Despite watching the other woman, she handed the two jade stones to Devlin. "What do you think, Teach, was I successful?"

"Um." He sounded nervous. "I'm sure you were. You're an expert, right?"

Next to her Balzeno guffawed. "No, youngling, this is nothing either of us have done. Treat us like any other student." He held his gems out as well.

"Right, of course, just like anyone else. I shouldn't treat the two of you like honored Elders, got it." He audibly swallowed as others started walking up. He turned to face a bit away from them, then focused on Betsy's stones. His head bobbed before he turned back. "These will work, but probably not as far of a distance as Violet's. It's hard to explain. It's like you fought the flow."

Betsy barked out a laugh. "Well, that's a fair assessment." She cut her eyes to Violet. "But Violet's gems were better?"

"Oh, yeah. Hers were nearly perfect. She has an affinity for gems. I think she should come to classes a few times a week. It would be nice to have someone I can train to help me teach one day."

A gasp preceded Violet gaping at him.

Warmth infused Betsy as she saw the shine of joy on Violet's face.

Devlin moved to Balzeno's gems. After a quick assessment, he nodded. "These are good. You could refine your etching, and we can discuss your symbol. There's actually an art to what you use. I think we could come up with ways to amplify the distance I'm sensing in your gems."

"Good, very good, youngling. I look forward to our talk."

A buzz at Betsy's side had her patting herself down. *Wait, didn't I turn off my phone?* She dug in her pockets and pulled out the jade stone Devlin had given her days ago. Waving to the others, she stepped back. "Hello? Viera?"

"Hiya, Betsy! I was playing a game with Scout and missed the first check-in. We're past the edge of the solar system, so you can let Devlin know that his gems are great. Their range is definitely farther than the range of the planet." She snickered. "It looks like you can hear me. I'll try again at the GPS before we go through, but this is amazing! I can hear you, you can hear me, now I'm going to go get dinner."

Betsy laughed. "Sounds like a plan. Actually, I think I want to get dinner, too. Safe travels and give Scout a hug from me."

She headed back to the new magic students, listening to Devlin speaking about how they did.

"...and Trinity, great work." Squinting, Betsy saw most of the people there were the younger wizards that had recently joined the school. "Your stones are really good, almost as good as Betsy's. I think with a bit of practice, you could move up to more technical types of gem imbuing." Devlin turned to the others. Though there was one teen in those assembled, it was mostly the adults. "As for the rest of you, I know you struggled and couldn't get the second gem to echo the etch you did on the first. I've asked some of the people back in Oz to create a spell in some paper that when you rip it, it will amplify your circle to duplicate your etching on a second gem. I'm hoping it will help you get a feel for what's supposed to happen. If this isn't successful, those of you who can't get the gem magic operational, I'll bring in others from town to work with you on tinctures and soap. I'll remind you, not everyone can do witch magic; we're just trying to open up new avenues of options. If this isn't your forte, don't worry."

I wonder if he's thinking about Dulaine and her inability to do witch magic. The whole town spent years thinking she was a magical dud, that is, until Balzeno came in and proved them all wrong.

The students nodded. All of this had been told to them in the past.

Once he finished, Betsy got Devlin's attention. "Viera just checked in halfway to the GPS jump."

His brows knit. "Okay, I'm glad her trip is going well. It was great having her here."

"No, Devlin, she checked in on this." She held up the communication stone.

Eyes growing wide, his mouth dropped open. "What? Really? off-planet?"

Betsy laughed, and Balzeno slapped him on the back. "Good work, youngling."

"Is she checking in again?" Betsy nodded as Devlin's words flowed together. He spoke fast, nearly tripping over his own words. "And you'll keep me informed."

"I will."

He nodded, then looked up as another student approached. He mumbled, "Thank you," before getting back to being the teacher.

Betsy rubbed Violet's arm. "Are you ready to head out? I'd like to get dinner, if you don't mind."

She nodded. "Sure, let's go. Devlin has one of the gems I made so we can figure out when I'll come here for more training."

The two walked away from the field, towards the spot used for transporting. "You really liked it, didn't you?"

"I did. It was fantastic finally being able to do some of the amazing things I get to witness all you wizards do."

A warmth filled Betsy. "That's great."

They got to the spot and typed on a panel Kafi had set up. Betsy whistled and a few moments later Wes and Buttercup swooped down, landing on her and Violet's shoulders, respectively. Then Betsy typed in her kitchen's location, and they were off.

"Where do you want—" The panel buzzed. There was a waiting message. "Hold that thought."

Betsy tapped and a message played, a low voice filling the space. "Hiya ... ah, Pillar Doeth, it's Toby, um, the fing, living out in Montana ... are you getting this? I haven't used my panel in ... well, right, why I'm doing this." He sighed. "Please contact me."

Betsy thought about the fing. He'd been hiding out on-planet for so long, isolated and alone, she often forgot he was here, an ambassador of his people.

Looking over at Violet, she rubbed her face, body shaking with mirth. "I tell you, Toby has been alone too long. Better give him a call before Bigfoot sightings pop up all over the place."

Betsy tapped the return call box, and a few moments later, Toby's voice boomed over the line. "Hello? Pillar Doeth?"

"Hi, Toby, I'm here with Major North."

"Major ... the chanzii representative? I thought she was a captain?"

"Hi, Toby," Violet said, her voice calm and welcoming. "I was recently promoted. Is it okay that I listen in?"

"Of course!" he said quickly. "I just, there was that thing in Montana last week. Can you fill me in on what occurred? I would like an update on what's been happening, please."

Betsy shut her eyes to think for a moment. "Sure. Major North and I were about to arrange for dinner, maybe—"

"Oh, perfect! Why don't you come to me? I'm cooking now. I can make enough for the two of you. I was planning elk with a huckleberry and balsamic agrodolce with a side of garlic mashed potatoes and, for dessert, grilled peaches with a huckleberry-thyme sauce topped with a sweet, clotted cream."

The fings were known for their cooking, and the more Toby spoke, the hungrier Betsy got. She watched Violet for her opinion, but by the end her eyes practically popped out and she nodded vigorously, a smile slowly spreading on her face.

"Sounds good, when do you want us?"

"Whenever you get here." He sounded happy at their quick agreement.

They decided to shower off the dust and grime of Africa before transporting to Montana. By the time they got there, the whole mountainside smelled divine.

They stood outside a dark cave that hid his perfectly respectable home. Anyone passing by would assume the crevice didn't lead anywhere—it was part of the magic used to keep Toby safe.

"Hello? Are you ready for us?"

"Friends!" Toby boomed. "Come on in. Dinner is almost ready."

Inside, the cave opened up to several large rooms with warm rugs and wood furniture. He had an overstuffed couch that faced his panel and a side table covered in books.

They sat at the oversized table, and Betsy felt like a kid again. He served them each a glass of wine—huckleberry wine—and returned to the kitchen to serve up the meal.

Once they were all seated, Betsy thought back on their trip to Montana. "When we last spoke, I told you about Oz and the city of witches."

Toby nodded. "Right, you now have two words that mean the same thing, but you are using them to mean different things." He sounded curious.

Betsy slumped and Violet laughed. After rubbing the back of her neck, hoping to stave off any headaches, Betsy sighed. "Yes, pretty much. The title 'wizard' has been universally used to describe anyone in the universe who had magic within them and could manipulate it. A wizard who can control a third type, or more, is titled an Elder."

Toby nodded. "Yes, all of this I know. But when you say witch, you're referring to something else."

Violet leaned forward. "I imbued a gem today, and I'm not a wizard."

Eyes wide, Toby's jaw dropped, and his back slammed the rear of his seat. "You did?"

"Yes!" A small giggle escaped her. "The Pillars have asked some of the witches from Oz to start teaching their brand of magic at the schools they're setting up—one in Africa and soon to be one in Australia. Anyway, we sat in on the first lesson, and, well, I did it. I used their method and created magic." Her hands flopped about for a few moments before she could continue. "It was just beyond amazing."

Toby's eyes got wide. "Can anyone do this witch magic?"

"No." Violet sipped her wine. "But it's something that more people can do than the wizard stuff. Maybe someday you can come to the school and give it a go."

Toby bobbed his head in thought.

Betsy took another bite of the elk, the flavors exploding in her mouth. "Do you ever eat anything that isn't huckleberry themed?"

"Why would I?" He sounded genuinely confused.

"Never mind." Betsy waved a hand. "Anyway. One of the children of Oz was kidnapped. We've been searching for her. There've been a lot of new wizards around the globe who have been picked up by nefarious groups. We thought that maybe one of them had her. At this point, none of our rescue missions have found her."

His face hardened. "What will you do next? Where will you look?"

She sighed. "I'm not sure. We won't give up until we find her, but we'll have to dig deeper. So far, nothing we've done has brought Dulaine back home."

Bugged

Viera

Tiffany and her parents walked up to the table. "Hi, Scout. Hi, Ms. Kor!" Her exuberance brought a smile to Viera's face but couldn't distract her from her whirling thoughts. Everything that dark elf and phoenix had said could mean only one thing ... they knew where Dulaine was. She'd sat there and listened while they spoke about sneaking their way onto Earth, to the town of Oz, to take Dulaine because they needed someone to train to imbue. Something about righting a wrong.

All that time on Earth searching had been for nothing. That elf ... Yav'til, had said he'd waltzed onto Earth and taken her weeks ago.

Viera shook her head, reminding herself Tiffany was there. She smiled just as Tiffany spoke again. "I'm so happy to see you both again. Is it time to head to Abritos?"

Trembling, Viera gazed from Tiffany to the girl's parents, and then down to Scout. "I'm so sorry, I have to return to Earth—we have to let Betsy know where Dulaine is."

Tiffany's mom stiffened. "What is this all about, human? Are you threatening us? And what is a Dulaine?"

Viera's mind whirled at the question, uncertain how to answer.

Scout's face scrunched up. "What are you talking about, Ms. Kor?"

"Didn't you hear those two speaking next to us? They were talking about Earth and kidnapping ... look, we don't have time for this, I need to talk with

Horax and Betsy." She got up and gestured for the others to follow.

When Tiffany's parents tried to speak with her or Scout had a comment, she just continued to walk, not wanting to slow down.

Back at the ship, Viera found Horax on the bridge.

"You're back! Great, did you find the cambpulpo family? Can we head out?" The large blue qynad turned from her, nodding at people on the bridge, who scurried to their stations. "You—"

"No, wait, stop." Viera put up her hands, heat of frustration surging through her. "Listen to me, please. We have to go back to Earth."

Horax grunted, then turned back. "You didn't find them? Did they send a message? Are they meeting us there?"

"No, Tiffany and her parents are—" She heard the door slide open and sensed Scout and the rest enter the bridge. "Just listen." She wanted to grab the qynad and shake him. He finally focused on her. "There was an elf ... a dark elf? On the promenade. His name was Yav'til—"

A gasp came from several people on the bridge. Horax practically froze in place. "Are you sure about that name? We heard the alarms a few minutes ago, but I never thought..."

"Yes, I mean, I'm pretty sure. He said something about creating—"

"Okay, yes, let's move on from what he did and tell me what happened." Horax became flustered, a state Viera hadn't seen in him.

"He mentioned traveling to Earth to take a girl who knew imbuing magic. Horax, he has Dulaine. He wants to train her and use her for her magic."

His eyes narrowed. "How sure are you of this?"

"Scout was there; he can tell you." She waved behind her at the others.

"Um, Ms. Kor ... I, um." He stammered and she looked back to see what was wrong. His hands were clasped behind his back and his head was bowed. Finally he looked up. "I didn't understand what he said, he was speaking in high elvish, the language of magic."

Viera gaped, unsure what to make of that. Finally she snapped her mouth shut and shook her head. "He was what, now?"

Scout shrugged. "I was just shocked that an elf was on Torville Station Number Six and speaking with a phoenix. The firebirds never come down from their perches. It wasn't that I understood him."

The full impact of his words struck Viera like a truck. She forced herself to move—she couldn't be in shock ... not when she knew where Dulaine was. "Well, I don't know. I understood him. He said he sent her to a planet ten or twelve days from here. He wanted to redo his mistake."

"Contact Pillar Doeth," Horax bellowed.

Viera took a shaky breath, glad the qynad believed her.

"What about us?" Tiffany's mom demanded behind her.

"Your room is set up to your specifications." Horax spoke to them with a decorum Viera didn't think she could've mustered. "Scout can show you the way. Tiffany can stay with you, or she can stay in her own accommodations next door to yours. Let Scout know on the way to your chamber."

"What about—"

"I'll be around to answer any of your other questions once we leave the station, Ms. Lilyfloater. For now, please let us get this resolved so that we can be on our way."

Both of the Lilyfloaters sniffed and turned, walking away with stiff backs. The octopus shifters hadn't changed, even after spending time on their home world. *I just hope that time didn't harm Tiffany at all, poor girl.*

Scout gave Horax a serious face. "I can make sure they know where to go, Horax."

"Thank you, son."

Scout beamed, then led the family away.

The tension dropped, but didn't fully dissipate, once the lift doors closed, and Viera could finally breathe again. A woman at the front of the bridge turned in her seat. "Pillar Doeth isn't responding to communications, sir."

Horax grumbled low. It sounded like rocks rubbing together. "Viera, you have that stone you were supposed to test out. Maybe try that now?"

Viera brightened for a moment, then drooped. The idea that a gem imbued by magic would work from this distance didn't seem at all feasible. It had also been several days to get from Earth to the space station. Would Betsy still be carrying the other stone? Doubtful and frustrated, she pulled the jade from her pocket and pushed a bit of intent into the stone. "Betsy, it's Viera. Can you hear me?"

There was no response, not that she expected it.

Someone on the bridge checked a digital display. "Try again; it's just after midnight in Wisconsin on Earth."

With a grunt of dubious doubt, Viera gave the stone another try. *How am I supposed to know if it's failing because of distance or time of day? And why aren't I more tired? I should be a dead teacher walking.*

"Hello?" A yawn could be heard emanating from her hand. "Viera? Is that you?"

"Holy hell Betsy? Can you really hear me?"

A moan, as if Betsy were debating what answer to give, vibrated over the stone. "Do you know what time it is?"

"Please, listen, this is really important. I need to know if you want me to return to Earth." Viera spent the next few minutes relaying everything she'd heard on the station, giving more detail than she'd even told Horax. Knowing the time back on Earth, she felt tired and drained, ready to drop by the time she was done.

"That ass!" Betsy, on the other hand, sounded wide awake. "You go home, friend. I'll let you know if we need more help, but we have a lot of assistance here. You return to Thorn. Oh, and Devlin will be thrilled to know the range on these stupid stones."

"They're not stupid, they're fantastic." Violet's voice was soft but could be heard just as clearly.

"Hi, Major North." Horax rumbled. "It's good to hear your voice before we head home to Abritos."

A sharp laugh preceded her response. "Hi, Horax. I assume the crew can hear me as well. Safe travels everyone."

There were a few catcalls then Viera heard Betsy say good-bye.

Viera shook her head. Part of her was thrilled to be going home, but another wanted to find Dulaine and know the girl was safe. "Okay, I guess I'm not heading back to Earth. I'll have Flower Prancer put me in the language box after I catch him up on everything. Safe travels and I'll see you all when we get home."

Home. When did home become this new planet? She answered herself. *When it came with Thorn and Scout, silly.*

A Tale As Old As Time

Betsy

Lying in bed, Betsy debated waiting for the sun to rise. Her body ached with fatigue. She hadn't gotten enough sleep, but she didn't think she could rest after the news Viera just shared.

A warm hand rubbed her forehead. "What are we going to do first?"

Something in Betsy relaxed hearing Violet planned to stick with her during this. If Dulaine had been taken off-planet, Betsy had a lot of plans to make to save her. She'd made a promise to the girl's parents, and she still planned to follow through with her word.

"I ... we." Betsy sighed. For too many years she'd been a lone wolf. As much as she loved being a pair, and she did, it would take her a bit to adjust her thinking. She blew out a breath and started over. "We need to start with the other Pillars. I think we should head back to Africa and speak with Kafi and Balzeno. Marco may be there. He said he'd spend some time helping with the school. Once we're up, dressed, and ready to go, I think everyone else should be awake."

Violet slipped from the bed, gathering an outfit. "So, are you going to send out a meeting request before we get ready?"

Already on her phone, Betsy just grunted. After hitting send for a Pillar meeting in three hours, she gathered her own clothes. "I set the message for five our time, that's seven in the morning in Brazil. I hope Marco is up. It'll be ten in Africa and eleven in London. And eight at night for Ania over in

Sydney. It'll be an odd time where she's not meeting early in the morning for her."

Violet laughed. "You spend half your time playing around with time zones. I get it, but do you have an app to help, or have you done it so much that you just know?"

"I mostly know. I do have a note on my phone in case I'm feeling tired and don't want to think about it, but usually I can just tell you the time in the major places I visit or with the people I speak with the most."

The two climbed into the shower. They started off with a hug. Then Betsy slid her hands down Violet's smooth back to massage her ass while she enjoyed a good-morning kiss. Betsy enjoyed the feel of Violet rubbing against her body and moaned. She debated more, but they were both too tired and she shifted to washing. "Later, when I'm fully awake to enjoy every inch of you."

Violet chuckled low. "Deal."

They went about cleaning themselves. Betsy poured some of the Liveliness Lather soap products she'd gotten from Shenel at the bath and body shop in Oz onto her loofah. She feared it had been too long without a full night's sleep for anything to wake her and make her 'lively.' The magically imbued shampoo and soap did its best to make Betsy feel human.

Once dressed, the two headed to the kitchen for a quick breakfast sandwich and some coffee.

Violet yawned. "That bath product was amazing. I wonder if I can learn to make that. Or maybe imbue coffee to make it more potent." She gazed down into her mug. "Can you imagine?"

Betsy laughed. "Alright, my witch extraordinaire. Let's put the ven outside to play and head to Africa." After the two playful pets were outside for the day, they punched in the school on the panel and were off. A few moments later, they landed to a cool African morning.

Violet looked around. "Where do you think everyone is?"

"Well, it's just after three ... so, eight. My guess is they're having breakfast."

The other woman lightly punched Betsy's arm. "Are you saying we could've just waited and eaten here?"

One of Betsy's brows rose. "Are you saying you don't want to have a second meal?"

Laughing, they walked into the school, following the sounds of people and the scents of food. In the cafeteria, Marco saw them and waved. "Betsy, Violet, what are you two doing here? It's the middle of the night."

They both just acknowledged him with a nod of their heads as they went to get some food. Someone had made blueberry French toast and sausage. After filling plates, they joined Marco, who sat at a table with Kafi, Balzeno, Pearl, Devlin, and Soleil.

Kafi narrowed his eyes. "You look barely awake. Let me get you coffee, and then you can tell me why you're here this early."

Once Betsy had finished her first mug, she leaned back and smiled at the others at the table. "Okay, if you'd saw your email, you'd know I called for a Pillar meeting in—" she gazed at her watch, "—just under two hours."

Both Marco and Kafi pulled out their phones. Marco scoffed. "Well, hell, I don't know if I would've been on email before then if you hadn't told me. Both Ania and Zuza have replied that they'll be there."

Kafi grunted, then pocketed his phone. "I would've checked. I always do after breakfast. Are you going to make us wait?"

Betsy's gaze cut to Pearl and she shook her head. "No. I want to get the ball rolling on this one. The sooner we get it all figured out, the sooner I can get off-planet."

That got everyone's attention. Marco's face tightened. "You plan on leaving? You're the face of our group, you can't leave. Who will take over the press conferences and deal with the government?"

Anger surged through Betsy—as if her movements were dictated by everyone else! "I guess all of you will have to figure this out because I won't be here." Her jaw clenched as she took a breath, willing her emotions to calm. Once she thought she could speak calmly she continued. "Telling Juk of my plans is on the list. I don't think anyone will have to deal with the government. I also don't think we need to do any more press conferences. If any more are needed, one of you can do it, or even Balzeno or Devlin. The point is showing people on the other side of the screen that there are people who aren't scared. I think we've done it."

Soleil shook her head. "It's also to answer all of the questions."

Devlin laughed. "We live in the time of short sound bites. Wouldn't making small videos that answered each question be more efficient and popular? The videos could be uploaded to all the different social media sites. The questions could be answered at any time without worrying about time zones or being caught off guard."

Betsy raised her coffee up to him. "All this from one of the least technical people I know. You could be the face of these videos. You've been at a press conference, the people know you. Kafi and the other Pillars can help you figure out the answers. When I'm around I can also answer some of the questions. We could even throw Xantay up unless she ends up wanting to come with me."

"Okay, stop, Elder Doeth." Balzeno's voice was low, but it cut through their conversation. "You've played with your message enough. Tell us what you know."

She bowed her head at the other Elder. "Very well. Early this morning, at just before two, I received a gem call from Viera."

Devlin leaned forward. "How far away was she?"

His enthusiasm, like a kid being gifted the latest and greatest toy, made everyone smile. Betsy reached across the table and squeezed his hand. "She was at Torville Station Number Six. Your gems are amazing."

The others who knew how far that was whistled. Balzeno pulled a jade from his pocket and gazed at it. "I'll have to study your magic more, youngling. That distance is remarkable." He turned to Betsy. "And you spoke in real time?"

"We did." She went on to explain why Viera had such urgency to get ahold of her.

After she finished, a tense silence settled over the people at the table. Then Pearl leaned forward. "I'm going."

Marco's head shook back and forth fast in a barely perceptible motion. "No, Pearl. It's dangerous and once you leave the safety of Earth, you won't have your magic to protect you."

Her face tightened. "Most beings up there," she pointed up towards the ceiling, "don't have magic, right?"

Closing his eyes, Marco looked pained. "Yes, but—"

"Then I'm going."

His arm slid across her shoulders. "Please, can we talk about it?"

"No ... maybe. Just ... she's my sister."

"I know." His voice was soft. "And Betsy is who I'd trust more than anyone in this universe."

Before they could continue, Balzeno cleared his throat. "Yav'til, you say?"

"That's who Viera told me she overheard. But she also said Scout didn't understand him."

"And he wanted to try again with the source beasts of the yonat?" He waved his hand before she could answer. "This is bad."

Pearl's brow furrowed. "Who is this guy? What's his story?"

Balzeno sipped his coffee, then nodded. "Many years ago, I was just a youngling myself at the time, my people and the elves were ... well, we were never friends, but we weren't enemies. The long-lived beings try to stay on friendly terms."

His head fell back as if he were gazing at the ceiling. Betsy thought his mind was much further away.

"My people traveled the universe more back then. We were curious and wanted to learn about the different aliens. We were the first to stumble upon your planet. That many years ago it was very different. I remember making first contact with the wizards. They were scared, but willing to learn. On our second trip—my parents were diplomats—we invited the dark elves to join us. We thought they may bring the message to your people better since they looked more like your people."

For a few moments Balzeno shook his head and rubbed his face. "It was such a big mistake, but there was no way we could've predicted it."

Kafi pointed to the coffee mugs. Several of the people nodded and he got up to get refills.

Devlin leaned on his elbows. "What could you possibly have done that was so wrong? Earthlings were so primitive all those years ago."

A small laugh barked out of Balzeno. "You have no idea. But despite your people's lack of ... everything, except fire and basic structures in which to live, you did have one thing that no other planet has."

Betsy couldn't think of it. "What could we possibly have, especially over two millennia ago?"

"Don't you know? You ride horses. I mean, other planets have tamed large beasts of burden but using them for single rider transportation isn't done. Yav'til was one of the dark elves that joined my group to meet the Pillars. When he saw how horses were used, he had a lot of questions ... he seemed very interested. Since everyone in the group had questions, I don't know that anyone noticed his interest. When we left, I returned home and began my intense study for my third magic. It was time for me to rise in my ranks, so to speak."

Violet finished her second breakfast, then tilted her head. "How long until everyone knew what he was doing?"

"That took time." Balzeno sounded sad. "I learned later that he knew of a planet with beasts similar to your horses. When he tested them, they'd even let him ride on their backs. But he thought it would be great to have even more ... maybe a raiding animal who knew defensive moves and how to fight. That way, at night, he could have a beast of burden who could also stand as guard. Someone to switch off with. This was only one of the benefits he spoke of. The problem was his skill in imbuing wasn't great."

Around the table, Betsy noticed everyone looked confused. Devlin asked, "Imbuing? What did they want to imbue into these animals to do? To be? Smarter?"

"Haven't you guessed?" Balzeno teased.

Betsy narrowed her eyes. "He tried to make the horses more independent, right? A partner in his travels. A beast of burden who knew when to throw a spell or fight, but not so smart it fought being a beast of burden."

"And this is why you're an Elder." The dwarf beamed.

"No, it's because I apparently passed a test I didn't know I was taking," she snarled, then laughed. "So, what, he wants Dulaine to help him make new yonat that are less onerous?"

"The beasts on Qazah, the planet I'm talking about, are called the tuvan. When the current yonat became what they are, they decided to separate themselves from what their base material had been to the extent that they changed their alien type from the tuvan to the yonat. It makes sense; they are as similar to the tuvan as you are to a gorilla."

Pearl stiffened. "You didn't answer her question. What does this dark elf want with my sister?"

"To train her and have her help him imbue with subtlety. It was never his specialty. Imbuing really is a dying skill in the universe." He smiled around the table. "Except for here, of course."

5

Task Force

Betsy

After breakfast, Pearl stopped Betsy. "I know your Pillar meeting starts soon, but I'd really like you to take my request to join you seriously. I don't know if I could sneak onto the ship, but if that is my only option, I may take it. She's my sister, Betsy."

"I know. The problem is, as Marco said earlier, once you leave Earth, you won't have your magic anymore."

Face set, Pearl narrowed her eyes. "I've been thinking about that. If I understand the message you've been telling everyone who will listen, each and every one of us *has* magic within us. It isn't a matter of if, it's a matter of when and how to get it to open up, to blossom, to allow us to use it."

A sharp pain started slicing its way into Betsy's brain. *If I could just snap and have anyone magical in the way of wizards, doesn't Pearl understand I'd do it in an instant, especially to some people I think would benefit from it?* Instead of answering, she just nodded.

"Okay, well, Viera had her magic 'turned on,' right?"

And there it is. "Yes, but that isn't something I can just replicate."

"You can't or you won't?" Pearl's voice snapped out, but there was a quaver to it. Her pain stabbed into Betsy like a knife to her heart.

"Did you ever hear the story about how Viera got her magic?"

"No. Not really."

"A bug, alien, big, and a bit iridescent, that had threatened to kill her with a bite, ended up biting her after she did what it asked. One of the krottel, the aliens that Thorn's people just reclaimed their planet from. Their hope had been to learn about Earth from Viera, but the bite had a side effect of opening up her magic instead of killing her. It left her confused and nauseous. You can ask her; she once told me she doesn't want to do the next stage of evolution because of how awful the bug experience was.

Pearl shook her head. "The krottel, the ones who invaded here, right?" The throbbing in Betsy's head got worse as she signaled 'yes.' A hopeful light brightened the other woman's face. "Are there any of the bugs still on Earth? Could we at least try?"

Betsy rubbed her temples. "No, they were all taken off our planet."

"Oh." Pearl's body folded in on itself. Her sadness wafted off her in waves, strong enough for even Betsy's low-level sensing to pick up. She gave Betsy a quick hug. "Tell Marco I had to go home, and I'll talk to him later." She turned away. "Bye-bye, Pillar Doeth."

Pillar Doeth? When was the last time she called me by my title?

Betsy, Kafi, and Marco sat at Kafi's desk, sharing the same camera feed. They could've used three computers, but none of them saw the point.

Ania didn't look happy. "So, who do you see going on this rescue mission with you?" She didn't sound happy, either.

A warmth infused Betsy. She hadn't yet stated her plan to leave. Of course, Kafi and Marco knew, but they were letting her impart her story as she saw fit. Ania knew she'd given her word and rescuing Dulaine would be important to her.

"Violet has volunteered. She even sent a message to Thorn asking if we could use one of her ships. If she says yes, we get an experienced crew. I want to speak to Xantay, I think she'd be useful to have along. Beyond them, Pearl wants to go. It's her sister."

Zuza shook his head. "It wouldn't be safe, not to mention, as a witch, I don't know if she understands how awful she'll feel as soon as she leaves the planet's blanket of magic. We hold some of it in us, but she'll be naked of magic.

It suddenly occurred to Betsy that Violet may suffer some of this now that she was doing some witch magic. She'd have to speak with the Major and make sure she understood the possible repercussions of her actions.

Betsy lifted her hands. "I know and I agree. I told the young lady all of this. The only thing is ... what if we took her to Grarrou, the qynad home planet, before heading to Qazah."

"To where the krottel are being imprisoned?" Ania shook her head. "Qazah, is that the tuvan planet? I've never heard of it before. Is that the one Elder Balzeno believes Yav'til took Dulaine to?"

"Yes."

The other woman sighed. "Talk with Pearl's parents. I, for one, think it's an awful idea, but I don't even like leaving Australia anymore."

Betsy and Violet stood by the panel, gazing at its black surface, debating where to go. Violet rubbed her shoulder. "It's been such a long day. We could go home and get some sleep."

"Gods, that sounds amazing. But, no, I need ... *we* need to go—"

"Betsy! Hold up, don't leave yet! Betsy!" Marco yelled from across the yard, running around the corner of the building. "Betsy!" As soon as he saw them, he slowed to a walk. "Oh, you're still here, good."

Her mouth quirked up on one side. "You do know you could've texted me, right?"

He shook his head. "This was faster."

"Whatever. What do you want?"

He took a few deep breaths. "During the meeting. Pearl. Are you really considering taking her?"

"I don't know." Betsy sagged. She barely had any energy left, and this wasn't helping. "I was debating heading to Oz now to discuss this with her and her parents. I know she's old enough to not need their permission, but Dulaine is their daughter, and they need to know. And if Pearl wants to go with ... that family is so close. I don't want two of their daughters disappearing into space."

His body tensed, hands fisted, eyes shut, then he shook himself out. "Right. Okay. When you get things arranged, I'd like to be considered for the trip. I know that you're strong and don't need more wizard help, but if Pearl is going, I think she'll need more help than she thinks."

Violet reached over to squeeze Betsy's hand. Even in her tired stupor, she understood the subtext of what Marco asked. "Does Pearl feel as strongly for you as you do for her? Two rooms? One room?"

He jerked back as if slapped. "No, it isn't like that. I really respect her."

One of Betsy's eyebrows rose along with her hands in a placating sign. "Fair enough. I'll take your request under advisement. We need to make sure there are enough Pillars left on Earth right now. So much is happening. But if the others agree..." She let her statement fall off. In the end, it wasn't her decision alone.

"Okay, that makes sense. I'll let you two go ... and Betsy, thank you." His body tensed once again, before he stepped in and gave her a hug. "Either way, I know you'll save Dulaine. You really are the best." Backing up, he gave her a lopsided smile, then turned to walk back towards the school.

Violet shook her head. "How is it he doesn't know what's going on?"

"He's young. I think all of us Pillars are programmed to be a bit naive in that way. Which reminds me." She turned to Violet, her mouth suddenly dry. "I've been wanting to tell you, I know it's too soon, and I'm really tired and I'll do this all wrong but thank you for being part of my life. You've brought something I've needed for years, something I didn't even know I was missing. At this point, I can't imagine—no, I don't *want* to imagine—not having you there to discuss my plans, even the silly parts of my day with. You are the bright spot I look forward to."

As she spoke, Violet's face softened and a huge smile spread. She reached out to take Betsy's hands, squeezing them tight. "I love you, too, Betsy Doeth."

In all her life, she'd never heard those words ... not with that intent behind them, and she wanted to yell with the sudden onslaught of happy emotions filling her. Instead, she pulled Violet in for a searing kiss. As it ended, she sighed in happy contentment. "I love you, Violet North."

They landed in a field outside of Oz. Betsy stretched, glad that August meant the weather wasn't too different in all these places. It was just after seven in the morning, locally. "We should get breakfast."

Laughter erupted from Violet. She tried to catch her breath, but then doubled over, unable to stop. "Fire clouds in the sky! How many times can we eat breakfast?"

"Don't you swear at me, young lady."

That set her off again and Betsy joined in. Violet wasn't one for exclamations, and that one wasn't really a swear, more like 'holy moly!,' but still, she must have been frazzled to say it. "Well, I want lunch, but it's early here, so ... breakfast, my hobbit friend."

Betsy got her breathing under control. "Breakfast it is. Afterwards can we head to

California for a fourth breakfast? Or maybe Hawaii?"

"Don't tempt me, you temptress!"

That got them both laughing again, and it took a few minutes before they could make their way to the local eatery.

After they'd had spinach and feta quiche, with more coffee, they made their way to Pearl's family's home.

Violet shimmied. "Do you think they had added some 'awake' power to that food? The longer I'm up and around the Oz folk, the more suspicious I am of everything they give me."

Taking stock of herself and her surroundings, Betsy realized she felt oddly awake, too. "That, or the coffee was just that good. Like you suggested yesterday ... today? This morning? Gods above, at some point, coffee with a kick."

Still bouncing, Violet hooked her arm in Betsy's. "This morning. Before we went to Africa. Today really has been forever."

When they got to the house, Betsy rang the doorbell. Porter, Pearl's dad, answered the door. "Oh, Betsy, Violet, what are you doing here so early? Does it have to do with the story Pearl's been telling us?"

"Yes, I'd like to give you all of the information before you as a family make any decisions. I hoped to be here when you learned about my call last night, but knew Pearl needed her family. I had to speak with the other Pillars to decide exactly what our plan of action would be. I didn't want to come with only a small bit of information."

As she spoke, the three headed into the living room. She and Violet sat on the loveseat and Vicki, Pearl's mom, brought them coffee.

I wonder how much I've had today? Is it enough to keep me up until tonight? Is it enough to keep me up until tomorrow night? I hope I don't start vibrating.

"I already told them you know where Dulaine is." Challenge burned in Pearl's gaze. "I also explained that someone from the family should be there so she knows we love her and isn't scared when she's rescued ... because we *will* rescue her."

A tension filled the room. Everyone turned to Betsy as if waiting for her to argue. She gazed into each of their faces. Pearl's was hard, ready for battle. The young woman wanted to be brought on this mission and had her game face on. Vicki looked pensive. She sat on the edge of the couch, wringing out her hands. Porter's worried expression bored into Betsy, begging her to fix his family.

"This trip will be dangerous. I don't know how long we'll be gone. From what Viera overheard, the trip will take about two weeks to get there from here. Once there, we have no idea what obstacles or combatants we'll face." She licked her lips and took a deep breath. "Once we leave Earth's orbit, all of us, we'll be cut off from magic. I don't know if you realized how debilitating that is."

"Pearl mentioned making her a wizard." Porter's low voice sounded pained. "Is that really a possibility or the flighty hopes and dreams of youth?"

"Dad!" she snapped out.

"No, Pearl, I need to get all of the facts." He sat up and faced his daughter, his voice stern, laced with emotion. "I know we can't make this decision for you, but if I'm going to lose both my daughters, I'd like to understand here and now."

Betsy lifted her hands. "Let me explain. The idea of making people into wizards is not something any of us have thought of before it happened to

Viera. When Pearl asked—demanded even—earlier today, I was dumbfounded."

"But—" Pearl's face morphed into one of pain and remorse, as if all her hopes were being taken from her.

"No," Betsy said, not willing to let the girl take over the conversation. "Let me finish." Once she knew the Katz family were focused on her and not Pearl's outburst, Betsy continued. "Last March, Viera ended up on a space station. It wasn't planned. Having never known about the world of magic or the actual existence of aliens, can you imagine how shocking everything was to her? More than that, all of us from Earth have a scent to us, something that some aliens can sense, a potential. The beings that attacked us—"

"The bugs?" Pearl asked, having heard this part of the story. "What did you call them? The krottel? Viera mentioned that they opened up her magic and pushed some of their sensing ability into her."

Betsy nodded. "Yes, the krottel. They did something to her to activate an evolution that changed her from average Earthling to wizard. After their attack here on Earth, they were banished to several different worlds. It was a punishment, taking away their ability for space travel. At the same time, it wasn't. They never really wanted to leave the confines of whichever planet they lived on. That's all they really wanted, a peaceful place to burrow and live a serene life ... as ironic as that sounds."

Vicki bristled. "I don't understand what all this history has to do with us and our daughters. So, the bugs are gone and Pearl can't evolve, we get it. Are you saying she can't travel with you, none of us can?"

As Betsy's muscles tensed, Violet rubbed her back and an unexpected harmony settled through her. *Is this what having a partner is all about?* "What I am saying is, during my discussion with the other Pillars, we decided that taking a detour to one of the planets the krottel were sent to would be worth the risk. We agree that Dulaine should have family around when she's rescued." Betsy decided that they wouldn't even entertain the idea that they wouldn't be successful. "But you have to understand, I ... we have no idea what will happen. The krottel may refuse. If they agree, the process may fail. And if it's successful, I don't know if Pearl will..." she faltered.

"You don't know if I'll survive." Pearl said, then bit her bottom lip. "It's playing around with bigger forces than anyone understands, and you don't know how I or my body will take to whatever it is these bugs did to Viera." A small smile played across her lips as she saw the looks on the faces of the adults in the room. "What, I have a medical degree. I understand the risks. I still think it's worth it."

Porter reached over to clasp Pearl's hand. "I don't want to lose you. I want both my daughters home and safe. I don't care about magic or any of it, I just want you both where I can snuggle you." Tears trailed down his face.

Pearl got up and gave her dad a hug. "I know. I want that, too. But I think me going along is the best plan. I don't know what Dulaine has been through or what's going on with her. I just know the sooner she's with family the better."

Vicki nodded, quick and small, her expression drawn and sad looking. She sniffled. "As hard as it is for me to say, I agree. And there's no one Dulaine loves more in this world than her big sister."

Turning to Betsy, eyes ablaze, a smile slowly spread across Pearl's face. "So, Pillar ... Elder Doeth, when do we leave?"

6

Every Girl's Dream, And Nightmare

Dulaine

The tea by the side of her bed was warm. Every morning it was warm. *How do they know when I'll wake up?*

Dulaine pushed herself to sitting and sipped her morning drink. As always, it was the perfect temperature. Closing her eyes, she did her morning prayers. *Is Pearl okay? Mom? Dad? When they took me, whoever they are, did they harm my family? My neighbors? Anyone else in town? Are the people of Oz safe?* She swallowed, realizing today was a bad morning for her thoughts. *Will I be okay?*

Her body began to tremble, and she debated lying back down. She knew it wouldn't help. She'd just wake up here again ... and again ... and again. Tears filled her eyes.

Shower. I need to wash away my emotions. I can hide in the shower.

She padded through the closet to the bathroom, selecting black pants and a light-blue long-sleeved top that would fall to mid-thigh. The clothing all fit and felt soft, like cotton.

Once clean and dressed, she walked out and found food at the small table. There was also a woman standing by a chair. A sense of peace followed her initial confusion at seeing a being for the first time. Then she tensed realizing the person was her captor and probably dangerous.

The woman was tall; she looked like a frail tree that could be blown over in a strong breeze. Her skin was a light purple and she had pointed ears.

Everything in Dulaine told her to run, but she'd searched the room every day since she'd arrived, and she knew there was no place to go.

"Good morning, young one, my name is Max'ina. Will you join me?" Her voice was light and airy. Her name, Max Ena, made Dulaine wonder if Max was short for something, something she didn't think Dulaine could pronounce.

"What are you? Why did you take me from my home? Where are we? Can I speak with my parents?" She didn't move. This was the first time she'd seen anyone since she'd been taken from her bedroom and she wanted answers.

The woman's face barely changed, but Dulaine saw the sides of her mouth tighten. It was the same tell her mom had when she was annoyed by questions from the crowd. "If you'll sit and eat, I'll try to answer as many of the questions as I can." There was a melodic, peaceful quality to the woman's voice begging Dulaine to do whatever she asked. It tugged at her soul.

Jaw clenched, Dulaine just gazed at her. Then she said, "You took me from my home in the middle of the night. You've kept me here for," she shrugged, "I don't even know how many days. And now you're telling me, Max Ena," she said each of the two names distinctly, "that you can't answer any of my questions before I sit?" She could hear the anger in her voice.

"Very well." Max, short for something, sighed. "I didn't take you from your home, someone I ... well, we'll just say I work for him, it's easier that way. He and I are," she shut her eyes for a moment, "I believe your people call us elves. We are on the planet Qazah, so speaking with your parents would be very difficult. And my name isn't Max Ena, it's Max'ina, one word. Now, I've answered your question, will you please come and eat?"

For a few seconds, Dulaine just thought about everything the elf had said, breathing deeply, letting the new information settle within her. Then she stepped forward. "So, you didn't take me? It wasn't your decision?"

"No, child. I was asked to help acclimate you to Qazah and introduce you to the tuvan."

Dulaine sat and so did Max'ina. "Why did you wait so many days to introduce yourself?"

"That is a good question. I am on very strict orders. I was told to make you comfortable and to not make contact. Yesterday, they changed. 'Talk with the girl, let her move around the area, and meet the tuvan.' That was it."

A thought occurred to Dulaine, and she didn't like it. "You're as much a prisoner here as I am, aren't you? You couldn't just up and leave, taking me with you?"

Without changing her expression, the woman tilted her head slightly. "No, child, I couldn't. It wouldn't fare well for me or my family. Now, eat, before the food gets cold."

Dulaine debated another few seconds, but hunger won out.

After breakfast, Max'ina produced a pair of sturdy boots for Dulaine, and the two left the suite of rooms she'd been occupying for ... *goodness, how long have I been here?* She shook her head, realizing she had no idea.

Once they got outside, she debated running, but the thick trees and the steep mountain side didn't give any indication of which way to go. Swinging her head, she didn't see any paths or roads.

"I know you want to run, but this is an uninhabited planet. You won't find anyone else to speak with but me. I don't know if you'd survive for long if you ran."

A sense of dread filled her. "Is this one of the dead planets?"

"Dead? I don't know what you're talking about."

"The ones that ..." She scrunched up her face, then shook her head. Betsy had told a story of planets dying. That was why aliens had come to Earth. But she couldn't remember any of the specifics. "I don't know the details. I guess with all these trees, it isn't dead. But why aren't there beings on it?"

Max'ina shrugged. "Either none evolved or they left. I don't know the history of Qazah."

They weaved their way through thick trees, avoiding thickets and fallen logs wider than Dulaine was tall. After almost an hour, they got to an open field. A shimmering rainbow of colors met her gaze. As she watched some unicorns, wait, not unicorns, yonat, ate grass, others ran, and a few lay in the sun relaxing.

She looked up at Max'ina. "Are we on the yonat home world? Aren't they beings that could help me? Is that why we're here? Can these Elders get me home?"

A sadness crossed Max'ina's face, and she huffed out a laugh. "Child, these beasts are no yonat, they are tuvan. Follow me."

As they entered the field, the brightly colored animals that looked like the unicorn she always dreamed of seeing in a field, all watched, unafraid.

Max'ina leaned down. "I've been coming out every day, bringing them treats. I didn't want them running away when you finally got to meet them."

They approached a bright green animal with a vibrant blue mane and tail. The horn was golden, as were all of the tuvan horns. Max'ina pointed with her chin. "Go ahead, see if you can get close enough to pet it."

Dulaine held out her hand. "It's okay, I won't hurt you."

The animal sniffed, then stiffened and darted away. A few others in the immediate area followed suit and Dulaine slowly lowered her arm.

"I was afraid of that. Here, take some of these balls. They are safe for the animals to eat. I hoped you could approach without the food, but apparently, I was wrong." Max'ina's face mirrored the disappointment in her words.

Smelling the balls in her hand, Dulaine could scent something that reminded her of a garden. The next tuvan was red with white and pink splotches, almost as if the printer ran out of ink when creating it. The mane and tail were as yellow as a sunflower. This time when she approached, one of the treats in her hand, the others pocketed just in case, the animal sniffed the air with interest.

For each step Dulaine took, Red, for that's how Dulaine thought of it, stepped towards her. It was like a silly dance that ended in Red eating and Dulaine petting. Red was soft and emanated a rumbling sound when she scratched its neck.

Another of the creatures, yellow with orange highlights, approached, and Dulaine gave it a treat as well. She spent some time petting and getting to know these two lovely beasts. Despite wishing she were home, a giddiness at being this close to the tuvan, being able to pet them, thrilled her.

After some time, Max'ina approached. "Do you want to see if they'll allow you on their back?"

"Isn't that disrespectful?" Dulaine remembered the stories from Betsy about not riding yonat. She didn't want to do anything to ruin this experience.

"No dear, these aren't the Elders. It'll be fine." Dulaine wasn't sure she believed Max'ina, but she agreed.

The elf, so frail looking, picked Dulaine up like she weighed nothing. She placed her on Red's back. The tuvan stiffened but didn't react in any other way. Dulaine saw Max'ina give the beast more treats.

They stayed there for a bit longer. A thrill surged through Dulaine.

I can't believe I'm sitting on a unicorn. My every childhood dream is coming true. Magic, a unicorn. If only Pearl were here to see me now. Oh, and if I could gallop across the field. Not that sitting here isn't amazing, too.

She pulled herself out of her musings when she realized Max'ina had moved from in front of Red. "You've done amazingly well today, child. Next time we'll try having the tuvan move with you on its back. Maybe you could even ride it around the field."

The words were so close to Dulaine's thoughts, she giggled.

Max'ina helped her down. "Now, child, let's go get some more food."

Dulaine followed, darting glances back at the field of dreams. "Why do you always call me 'child'? I mean, I know I'm young, but I do have a name, you know."

"I don't know, actually. You never told it to me."

Dulaine's jaw dropped. *Why did I think she knew? It's not like I'm some famous kidnapped victim.* "Oh, sorry." She turned and held out her hand. "Hi, Max'ina, my name is Dulaine, it's ... well, not a pleasure, I'd rather be home, but it's nice to meet you."

A smile spread on Max'ina's face. "It's nice to finally meet you, too."

If It Weren't For Red Tape, Would There Be Tape?

Betsy

Walking through the entry of the government building Monday morning, Miranda smiled at them. "I brought you both coffee and fruit tortes. They looked so good this morning, I couldn't help myself."

Betsy groaned. "You know you don't have to spoil us," her hands snapped out to grab everything before Miranda could pull the items away. "Not that I'm saying 'no.'"

The receptionist smiled. "Every time you come, Juk ends up annoyed and frustrated. Trust me, it's worth it to all of us. You bring him down several pegs. The rest of the staff have started a fund for your meetings. Everyone wants you to continue to come in regularly until he's trained and less ... you know, him." She finished her statement, waving her hand in a circle in his general direction.

Both Betsy and Violet laughed, taking their goods and heading to the conference room. Juk wasn't there yet, and they each ate a torte.

Violet moaned. "It's worth it just for these. And knowing why she brings them, priceless."

A smile spread on Betsy's face and she leaned over to give Violet a quick kiss before the onerous man showed up.

She'd finished her pastry and was halfway through the coffee when the door opened. "Oh, I am so sorry I'm late. You know how it goes."

"No," Betsy said, her face blank. "I don't. From what I remember from our previous meeting, you were told that we're your top priority. You were to be here prior to my, and if Major North joined, our arrival. We are discussing not only international issues, but intergalactic issues. If you have something more important, please, let me know. I'll speak with Orson and find a replacement, one that won't leave us sitting here for a quarter of an hour waiting."

His mouth opened and closed like a fish out of water before he made to grab the bag for a treat.

One of Betsy's brows rose. "You were late, you do not get one of these. Now, Juk, do you have anything to bring to this meeting, or will it just be me letting you know about my side of things?"

He chuckled. "Do you have that much to share, Betsy? I really feel like you give me and my team things to do and sit back waiting for our reports. Aren't these meetings more about me filling you in?"

She continued to stare at him, waiting. After a few seconds he began to squirm. "Right." He opened his leather folder and looked over his notes. "The men you brought in from one of your raids, we've gotten them to speak. We know more about the overall plan to get magic users. We're setting up more rescue missions. Should I assume you want to be part of those?"

"No. Anything else?" *I wonder if I could convince everyone to let Xantay take over these meetings. Maybe if he annoys her, she'd just eat him.*

His brows rose, then he consulted his notes. "We don't have any more press conferences scheduled. Is that something you want to continue?"

"Again, no. I have spoken with Devlin and a few of the others. He has a better idea of how we can get the information out. Please get over to the African school in the next week and speak to him. I think Devlin would be a great lead for the project."

Juk's eyes narrowed. "Not you or one of the other Pillars?"

"I'm the only Pillar who has been on camera. I am planning a trip off-planet that will take over a month. During that time I won't be able to work on the project. Devlin was at the last press conference, so he is a known entity. His plan is for asynchronous videos, so anything asked, he can answer. The other Pillars can help with forming the answers."

Juk sputtered as he spoke. "You're planning what? We have so much going on right now. People have just learned about magic and aliens, and the girl you promised to find. I can't imagine what would be so important that you'd just drop all your responsibilities and trot off on a pleasure vacation. I don't think I can approve such a thing, Betsy. No, not possible."

As hard as she tried, it was too much, Betsy laughed. Violet covered her mouth to keep from making noise as she chuckled, too.

"I fail to see what's so funny," Juk snarled.

Betsy held up both hands and shut her eyes. She couldn't look at him and get control. After a few seconds, she felt the need to giggle finally subside. When she opened her eyes it tickled the back of her mind, but she pushed it down. "Juk." She took a breath as his glare deepened. "I appreciate that you believe you have any control or authority over me or any of the Pillars, but, in the kindest of terms, you can fuck the hell off. Your dictates over my actions, to put it mildly, don't mean a thing. Now, my control over your job is pretty much absolute. You should *finally* get that through that thick head of yours before I do follow through with my threats and start over with someone new."

She leaned back, watching the series of emotions play over his face. Sipping her coffee, she wondered if she'd pushed him too far.

Violet leaned over. "Is he going to be okay? His face is turning purple."

Betsy shrugged. "Now, if you want to start over, I'll tell you about *why* I'm heading off-planet, which is what you should've asked. Your disrespect is getting overwhelmingly obnoxious. I tire of desiring respect and getting, well, you."

The snap of Juk's jaw snapping shut echoed in the room. He took an audible breath through his nose then nodded. "Please, Pillar Doeth, tell me what is *so* important off-planet, you feel taking over a month away at this point is in all of our best interests."

She sighed. "That really wasn't better. I'm going to suggest to Orson some interpersonal training for you while I'm away." She watched as his face scrunched up even more, though he didn't say anything. "I received a message from Viera at just before two in the morning Sunday. She'd made it to Torville Station Number Six. While there, she overheard the discussion between a dark elf, a male that has been on the run with a bounty on his head from just about every civilized world for almost two millennia, and a phoenix. During their conversation, the elf explained how he'd come to Earth to steal away a child with the ability to imbue and take her to another planet."

"But that's Dulaine!" Juk all but shouted.

Betsy sighed heavily. "Yes. We know. I spent the next eighteen hours getting the story of this dark elf, planning with the Pillars, talking with Dulaine's family, and arranging exactly what a rescue mission would look like."

"Are you saying this elf is two thousand years old? That isn't possible." Juk gazed at them as if they both had lost their marbles.

"No, it isn't possible for most humans to be that old. For the long-lived beings—elves, dwarves, krottel, and the like—it is very possible." She held up her hands to stop him from saying more. "I believe I have created a group to go on this mission to save Dulaine."

Juk smirked, as if he had found a fatal flaw in her planning. "And how will you get to Dulaine?

The Ziner isn't in orbit. Or are they returning from that space station?"

Violet leaned forward, taking the bag and noisily searching for a pastry. She pulled out the last fruit torte and hummed. "These are simply amazing. You should ask Miranda where she gets them. It's like magic how good they are." She took a bite and moaned.

As she leaned back, enjoying the treat, Juk's eyes widened. "You asked Miranda to bring in treats for the meeting? Why aren't you sharing?"

"No," Betsy laughed. "She brought those in for me as a thank you. I didn't request anything. I'm not on site or arranging the meetings. *You* should be doing the meeting planning, including coffee and pastries, especially if it's something you want. As I mentioned before, you should also be here at least five minutes before us, if not more. If you don't know the basics of how to run a meeting, I'm sure Miranda could give you a binder with rudimentary protocols. If you're treating other clients like you are us, I wouldn't be surprised if we start to lose clientele. Do not miss my usage of the word 'we.' I am still your boss. Don't take any of these suggestions as optional."

Violet sipped her coffee and smiled. "Now, back to your question, which you should've asked me, being the chanzii representative in the room." One of her eyebrows rose. "I've requested a ship from Abritos. I know it will take some time for everyone to get their proverbial ducks in a row before we can leave. If Thorn says yes, that's what we'll use. Otherwise, I'm pretty sure Toby has a ship in orbit, as does Xantay. Though hers is small, we can make our first stop at her home planet to change to a bigger one."

Juk gaped ... again. "Xantay is going with you? Is Balzeno going, too?"

"Xantay is going for a few reasons, but no, *Elder* Balzeno wants to help at the school in Africa. He plans on staying."

"Who else will travel with you?"

It's about time he treats this like a conversation and not try to bully us. Betsy smiled. "Violet will go as pilot. She knows how to fly almost anything. Xantay wants to help if there's anything dangerous where we end up. The elf we're facing has been on the run for a very long time; we don't know how dangerous it'll be. Pearl plans on coming with so that when we save Dulaine she has family to help with any trauma."

Juk nodded. "I don't love the idea of Pearl joining, but I'm guessing that conversation has come and gone. Are any of the other Pillars going?"

Betsy thought about Marco and his request to join the mission. "I'm not sure at this moment. My presumption would be 'no,' but I'll keep you informed if that changes."

"Very good. Then, since I'm guessing this is the last of these meetings for a while, I'll see you when you get back."

She nodded. "You will."

"And keep the reports coming, Betsy. Don't forget us on your joyride across the galaxy." The door shut before she could respond.

Violet chuckled. "He is such an ass."

Your Ride Or Mine

Betsy

Warm, hot kisses trailed down Betsy's neck. A shiver shot through her body and she arched up, waking with a moan. "Gods above, tell me I'm not dreaming."

Violet's slick tongue traced circles just below her shoulders before she blew lightly. "Hush, let me have my appetizer. I let you sleep for a few hours, behaving admirably, I might add." Betsy didn't see Violet, hidden behind a waterfall of dark hair, dip down. There was no warning before Violet devoured her left breast.

Trying to breathe, to think, Betsy lost herself in sensations. Violet put a leg between hers, rotating her hips to give them both friction. Betsy lifted a knee, giving Violet something to rub against. A free hand clasped her right breast, circling the tip.

Teeth lightly scraped up, tugging Betsy's nipple. Pleasure built within her. When she ran her nails down Violet's silky-smooth back, the other woman bit down slightly harder. Betsy gasped, bucking up.

Violet pinned her down, moving up to join their lips in a searing kiss, rubbing their bodies together. Her fingers lowered, finding Betsy's clit. Betsy rubbed down, sliding from Violet's back, but the sexy vixen pulled up from the kiss. "No, leave your hands on my back. If they go anywhere without my permission, only one of us will find our release." A slow smile spread across her face and her eyes shone in the waning light. "Do you think you can follow that one rule, Elder?"

Her voice did things to Betsy. It had been years since anyone had spoken to her with such authority, and she sank into the submissive role. Digging her fingers into Violet's soft skin, she allowed a smile to curve across her face. "Yes. I think I can."

With a speed she could hardly follow, Violet dipped down to nip at Betsy's neck, then kissed her way back up to her ear where she traced the outside, before sucking the lobe. She continued to stimulate Betsy's clit, every now and then slipping down, dipping into her.

"You are wet, but I'm guessing I still have time to play." There was a wicked edge to the alien's voice. Despite thinking it didn't sound good for her future, Betsy groaned in anticipation.

Once again, Violet kissed her. Betsy's body bowed with the sensations surging through her body.

With a deep rumble that sounded like disapproval, Violet began moving down Betsy's body. She got to a point where Betsy didn't think she could keep her placement on the other woman's back. Quivering with need, Betsy used her ab muscles, currently being nibbled on, to sit.

Violet chuckled, then shifted, sliding her hands around Betsy so their legs were intertwined, and their slickness met. Their bodies stimulated by continuous touch and movement.

Betsy shifted to grasp Violet's luscious ass as Violet's hand moved between their bodies. "I don't know which of us is slicker. But soon it'll all be one, my sexy human."

As Violet performed magic, she gasped. "You're cheating, but gods above, don't stop!"

One hand low, the other high on Violet's back, Betsy held her close as her body tightened. The orgasm building with each flick, rub, and probe.

Smiling wide, Violet said, "Scream for me, Betsy!"

As her world fractured, Violet caught her mouth in another kiss, her body trembling with the waves of pleasure. The play of Violet's fingers continued as Betsy thought she may fly into space, here and now, without a ship.

Betsy felt when Violet orgasmed. She reveled in the sexy alien's gorgeous release. It almost caused her to peak again. And then the two flopped back down, smiling at each other like goof balls.

A yawn overcame Betsy and she stretched. "That was amazing. The perfect wake up."

Violet smiled. "Shower. Then we can figure out dinner. After that ... gods, I can't think."

Betsy stood and headed for the bathroom. When she got there, she realized she was alone. "You're not joining me?"

"I mean, if you think you'll fall asleep, but otherwise no. You first. I'm going to check in with work and be down afterwards. You decide on food. Surprise me."

"Sounds good." After her shower and getting dressed, Betsy headed to the kitchen. Again, she marveled at how much she adored having the other woman in her home. Betsy never thought she'd want to share her space, but now she wondered if she could imagine not having the vibrant Violet there, stimulating her mind and body.

At the panel, she ordered two mugs of tea. While she waited, she pulled out her phone to see if she had any emails she'd missed that day. In her email, she found a group message from Marco.

Hi, everyone,

I spoke with Betsy about her trip. I think I should be included on the roster. I know she and I have the same two proficiencies, but having a bit more magical oomph wouldn't be the worst idea.

-*Marco*

Though Betsy had her opinions on the matter, she decided to wait on voicing them. She'd respond in the morning, give others a chance to chime in.

There were a bunch of junk notices. Some she deleted, some she unsubscribed from. *I swear I unsubscribe every other week to some of these.*

There was an email from Orson. A sigh escaped her before she could stop it. "Did Juk cry to daddy?" she mumbled to herself.

Betsy,

I hear you're going off-planet to save the young lady from Oz. I'm glad to hear you got a lead on where she ended up. I want to say I was as worried as you were over her safety, but I'm not sure that's true. You knew her and know the family. Though her safety is very important to me and her rescue is a top priority, in the end, she is still little more than a name on a page.

Before you leave, I would love for you to come visit. I'd like to work through some of the logistics of the trip. I know you've discussed some of this with Mr. Hopkins, however, as you know, some of the details can get lost in translation with our fledgling Juk. He is coming along in his training, but he's still young.

I'll expect you at nine on Friday, unless you tell me otherwise, and let me know if you'll be bringing Major North or anyone else with you. I'll have Chef prepare a brunch meet and greet.

As always, yours,

Orson

Betsy smiled at the formal letter hidden in an email. "I wonder if he even knows we've entered the digital age?"

"What was that?" Violet said as she entered the kitchen.

"Oh, nothing. I was musing about Orson." She stood and engulfed the beautiful alien who'd captured her heart in an embrace. "Let's go paint this town red!" she said, smiling big enough to hurt her cheeks. The sensation so new, it confused her. "How about we find a nice Italian restaurant, then take a walk on the path by the lake?"

Arms still locked around Betsy's waist, Violet leaned back to gaze into her eyes. "That sounds perfect. Now, I didn't drive here, so either you're driving or we transport to my place, and I drive."

"Hmm, your ride or mine? Well, you live closer to downtown. Why don't we take yours?"

"Sure!"

They transported to Violet's and then drove to a nice restaurant, quickly deciding on what they wanted to order.

Betsy sipped her wine. "Anything interesting in your messages from work?"

"No. Everyone seems excited to have a timeline to head home to Abritos. The group who have petitioned to stay here is much larger than I thought it would be. I'm compiling a list of names, locations, and occupations. I'll send it to Juk for final decisions once I've given my recommendations to Thorn and she's okayed it."

"Do you want me to start the internal team thinking about numbers? We can't have the other alien races claiming preferential treatment, even if the chanzii ended up here for legitimate reasons. Would that help or hinder your job?"

Violet bit her lip. "I'm not sure. Let me think on it. If you give me a number much smaller than those who want to stay, that would be rough. In that scenario, I'd rather not know, you know? Just give the list over and hope your people change their mind.”

“Ask for forgiveness instead of permission?”

“Exactly!” Violet held her glass up for a clink.

“Besides the ones who want to stay, the others are okay with the lottery system for exiting the planet?” Betsy could just imagine the infighting to get home.

“Mostly. I’ve set up a priority for people who have jobs that would help rebuild Abritos. Their likelihood of selection is higher than the average citizen, though everyone is in the lottery. The people who were critical are already gone.”

“All your people are so busy. Is there a slow period for a few months while the rebuilding happens?”

“Thorn said most of the buildings and land were still intact. We all thought that the time between the krottel leaving and us returning would be years, but my guess is, by the end of this year we’ll be in serious relocation mode.” Her eyes shone with excitement. Even though Violet was not leaving Earth, Betsy knew she loved the idea of her people getting their planet back.

A server approached. Betsy's chicken parmesan and Violet's lasagna both looked and smelled amazing. "Would you like fresh grated cheese?"

"Yes." Betsy nodded. "Thank you."

Violet also confirmed she wanted some too, and then they dug in.

The two were quiet for a few minutes. Then Violet's head snapped up. "Oh, I can't believe I forgot. Thorn sent an email. After speaking with us, Horax sent her a priority message. She agreed with the urgency of the situation and arranged a ship to be sent. Once it's here, it'll be mine for the duration of this mission."

Relief washed through Betsy. "That's fantastic. If she got the message on Sunday morning and sent the ship right away, it should be here by next weekend. We may be able to leave early next week."

Violet nodded. "I agree. Our plans can really come together."

A Shift In Perception

Dulaine

The tea sat right where Dulaine expected it, warm and inviting. She swung her legs over the side of the bed and smiled, bringing the mug to her face and breathing in the alluring scent. The open screen walls of her room meant she was closer to nature but also exposed to the cooler night air.

After she finished drinking her morning brew, it felt like tendrils of warmth spread throughout her body, preparing her for the day. She sighed and headed to the bathroom. Along the way, she selected dark green pants that reminded her of the leaves in the trees, and a multi-shade blue top.

Dressed and ready for the day, she found Max'ina waiting for her with pancakes and sausage. "Are you hungry, my young friend?"

Dulaine felt like she was forgetting something, but she wasn't sure what it was. The same thought had been bugging her for a few days, and she knew it would come to her soon, but for now, she liked having a routine.

"Yes, thank you." She smiled as she sat. "Are we going to go and see Red and Sunflower again today?"

The elf smiled. "Of course, Dulaine. It makes you happy."

Every day since meeting the tuvan, she and Max'ina had spent their mornings bonding with the wild beasts. Red and Sunflower, the yellow tuvan with orange highlights. The others in the field didn't seem to mind their intrusion, but they also didn't join in their unicorn games.

So far, only Red and Sunflower had taken to eating snacks from her hand and allowing her to ride them. She'd even begun to steer them with a bit of pressure of a heel and her knee on their side. Max'ina taught her how to control them this way.

After the hour hike, something else Dulaine was getting used to, they approached the field. For the first time, Sunflower trotted up, whickering a 'hello.'

Max'ina placed a hand on Dulaine's shoulder. "This is wonderful. This one likes you so much, it's approaching you before you even offer the treat. Ya ... You wouldn't think it would happen that fast."

At her stumble of words, Dulaine wondered what Max'ina meant to say. Was she about to reveal the name of her captor? Was she going to slip into a different language? How did Max'ina know English so well?

Before she could ask, Max'ina gave her arm a squeeze. "Why don't we start with you riding around the field? See if you can do that without a treat at all."

Excitement nearly exploded from Dulaine as the two approached the tuvan. *This would be amazing to share with ...*

"Okay, young friend, let me lift you up." Max'ina slid her hands around Dulaine and the next thing she knew, she sat atop Sunflower.

The wild creature was thinner than any of the horses Dulaine had ridden back—

Her thoughts were interrupted when Sunflower began to trot. "Whoa, I'm going to fall off with all this bouncing."

The tuvan sped up, finding a smooth canter to circumnavigate the field and the other tuvan. Dulaine began to giggle, not believing how much fun she had riding. She squeezed her legs to maintain her perch, and tried to move with the motion, not wanting to hurt herself or Sunflower. This wasn't the first time she'd ridden, but she hadn't done it much.

It didn't take long to get back to Max'ina, who smiled wide, pride clear in her demeanor. Once they stopped, Dulaine swung her leg over and slid down. She wobbled a bit with sore legs but didn't fall. Sunflower's fur was soft and she petted her friend, excited about their quick jaunt.

"Can I give her a treat, now?" Dulaine's hand dug in a pocket, finding one of the goodies the wild animals loved.

"Of course. Sunflower did an amazing job keeping you from falling. A treat is well deserved."

After that, the three walked around the field, their pace much slower. When they got near the other tuvan, Red trotted over to join them. As they walked, Dulaine switched from scratching one beast to the other. She gazed around, looking through the trees, up and down the mountain, depending on which side of the clearing they were on. At one point, she saw a small path. It seemed to run fairly flat.

Squinting, Dulaine tried to see how far it went. *I wonder if it eventually goes up or down. Is this only for animals or are there really other people, or elves, or—something—on this world?*

The two spent more time with the animals. Dulaine got to ride on Red, though the experience wasn't as smooth. After a couple of hours, Max'ina gave a curt nod. "I think it's time to head back into the house. It's an hour walk and you need to eat. What do you think? Are you hungry? Are you getting a bit chilly?"

A shiver ran down Dulaine's back. It occurred to her that she should've worn a jacket. Wasn't that something people usually reminded her to do?

She shook her head. *What is it I keep on forgetting?* "Would it be okay if I stay out here a bit longer? I'll come in soon; I just love watching all the tuvan and their pretty colors."

Max'ina's face tightened. "I don't like you out here alone."

"I'm not, Red and Sunflower are here with me. They won't let anything happen to me. And didn't you tell me there weren't any other beings on-planet? Isn't it safe?"

The tall elf sighed. "You'll stay in this field?"

Dulaine shrugged. "Where else would I go? The café?"

"What's a café?"

Dulaine smiled. "Never mind. I'll tell you over lunch. That'll be ready in an hour or so?"

The elf squinted, as if she were trying to figure Dulaine out. "Yes. That sounds right. I'll see you then."

A sense of freedom washed over Dulaine, quickly followed by elation, then dread. She shook her head. *Where did that last emotion come from? Why would I be upset about being outside alone? Is this the first time an emotion or thought has confused me?*

Once Max'ina was out of sight, Dulaine slowly circled the field. About a quarter of the way around the oval space, she found the path. She began walking it. The trees were close on both sides, shrouding her in cool darkness. "I really do wish I had a jacket."

There wasn't much to see as she walked—trees, tall and majestic, and a path, that led more or less straight from the field. The bushes and shrubbery were all cleared away, as if whatever wildlife used the path rubbed or ate the wild plants down, which was good since it all grew taller than Dulaine.

Birds sang a happy song, which lightened her step, and she wanted to whistle, but she couldn't remember any songs. *Why can't I remember—*

Between one step and the next, her world crashed down, a weight on her mind, body, and soul. She fell to her knees and cried.

Pearl! Mom! Dad! How could I have forgotten to worry about you? Have you forgotten about me as well? Where have all my worries gone? How have I been so ... happy?

Tears burned down her face, and she trembled as sobs escaped her body, carrying days of pent-up worry and the shame she felt for forgetting the people she loved most in this world ... well, on Earth.

A fuzzy nose bumped into Dulaine, and she realized Red had followed her down the path. She shifted to sit on her butt and scratched Red's nose, her hand shaking and cold. "What happened to me, Red?" Her voice came out weak and she sniffled. "Why did I forget all about my family, my town, Earth? What could've made my only thoughts be on you and this place?"

Dulaine slowly pushed herself to her feet and gazed up the path. She knew she had to get back to the house. She didn't want to end up locked up in that room again. *What if I lose the small freedom I've gained?*

The first step back towards the field felt like a punch to the gut. She didn't want to return to her imprisonment. *But where else can I go? How would I survive on this planet alone?*

Another step.

Dulaine shook her head. "What is wrong with me? I have unicorns and food and a roof over my head. I'm being such a drama queen! Goodness, I do *not* know what just happened."

When she looked down the path, Red still stood a few feet away. "Come on, silly creature, Max'ina is making lunch! We need to get back. What are you waiting for?" She stepped towards Red, and again, her memories slammed back into her. A weight that crushed her to the ground and she panted on her hands and knees.

After a few moments, she shook herself out and stood. "Right, magic. I live in a world where unicorns are real, magic is real, and elves kidnap kids from their families. She's doing something to my mind, like blocking my emotions, my memories.." She gazed over her shoulder down the path. "I'm guessing it's some sort of mind magic? Maybe life magic, if I remember my lessons from Elder Balzeno and Betsy. Do you think it's Max'ina? I guess it would have to be. Gah! She seems so nice."

Jaw clenched, Dulaine looked around. She found a small stone, barely bigger than her thumb nail. Sitting on the ground, she thought of the things Elder Balzeno had taught her. *Think of my want, my desire, form it into my intent, mix it with my well, and push it out into the item.*

"I don't have a lot of time, Red, I hope this works." She shut her eyes. *I need you to become a mind shield. Nothing can touch my mind.*

Red nosed her as she performed the spell. She reached out and placed her hand on the sweet beast's nose, rubbing. Then, focusing on the stone, repeated her will three more times, needing this stone to protect her mind.

10

The Final Roster

Betsy

The phone buzzed, dragging Betsy from her sleep. She groaned, pushed up from the bed, and glared at the evil device.

The week had been hectic. There had been people from all over the world who wanted information on joining the magic schools, and their availability wasn't always convenient. She had the most time of all the Pillars this week, so she'd been zooming all over collecting new wizards, and trying to get as much done as she could before leaving Earth.

Since Violet would be captaining the chanzii ship, she had been tying up loose ends, attempting to make her absence as painless as possible. She'd spent her time working day and night organizing her job, trying to head off any potential complaints that could arise in her absence. Because she wanted to be available to any one of her people before handing over control to her second, she'd stayed at home, just as hectic and busy as Betsy.

Rushed texts flew between them whenever they had time. Betsy still missed having her around.

Betsy rubbed her face, sitting cross-legged in the center of her bed. "I haven't seen anyone outside of new recruits, save Kafi and Marco since Monday. I feel like I'm already on a trip away from my regular life, except for my few hours of sleep every night at home," she mumbled to herself, stretching with a big yawn. "Gods above, I'm tired."

Her phone began to buzz again. She glared at it and was disappointed when it didn't quiver in fear.

The clock next to it flipped to eight forty-one. "Damn! I have to be at Orson's place in less than twenty minutes."

With more energy than she really had, Betsy pushed up from bed and gathered clothes. In the bathroom she brushed her teeth and washed her face. Her body, leaden with fatigue, drooped. She leaned heavily on the counter until done.

Though she loved jeans, going to visit Orson was more of an ordeal. She wore dark wine slacks and a sleeveless pale pink knit top with an oval cutout and a large decorative white button on her left shoulder. Once her hair was presentable, she made her way to the kitchen. The scent of coffee nearly lifted her off her feet, dragging her towards its heavenly seductive aroma.

Shaking her head, Betsy tried to get her brain back online. "Whoever broke into my home and made me the elixir of life, just know, once I grovel at your feet in gratitude and drink said mana of awakeness, I'll be able to take you down with my superior magical fighting skills."

A low, sexy laugh made its way right to Betsy's soul and she moaned. "Violet, you're cheating."

"You're the one who didn't answer your phone ... twice. I worried you were dead Elder sleeping, unable to wake. I came to get you out of bed, but your bed was empty when I checked, so I figured you needed coffee."

Betsy went to hug the other woman. It was more like collapsing into her, but since Violet didn't complain, she figured it was fine. "Thank you."

Pulling away, she picked up the mug and sighed at the heavenly, earthy scent. As she slowly sipped the brew, Violet chuckled. "Don't forget we have about two minutes to get to Orson's place."

Lost in the wonder of coffee, Betsy grunted. When the mug was almost empty, she put it down on the counter, smiled at Violet, and nodded. "Okay, let's go." Her brain finally somewhat working, she noticed the light purple dress Violet wore. "You look great, by the way. Sexy enough to lick."

Violet's step faltered. "Thank you." She gazed over her shoulder. "We'll do that later when I know you won't fall asleep mid-nibble."

Betsy chuckled, then yawned, ruining any bit of flirting she had started off doing.

At the panel, Betsy dialed up Orson's landing area, and the two were off.

"Is this how you eat every meal?" Violet asked, taking another bite of eggs benedict. She gazed at the massive number of plates littering the table. There were only three of them, but Orson had outdone himself with variety. He loved hosting a meal and spoiling his guests.

He laughed. "No, this is a special treat for my favorite Pillar and her guest. I know there's a lot, but once we're done, most of these items can be packed up for you to bring on your trip or saved for another meal for my staff. Either way, none of it will go to waste."

For a bit, the three just enjoyed the food. Betsy closed her eyes to enjoy the flavor, then jerked as she felt herself doze. She shook her head and took a sip of her coffee. She thought about how tired she was and knew she needed to be more alert.

Violet rubbed her leg. Betsy gave her a small smile before leaning back and gazing across the wide table. Across from her, she saw Orson's head tilted and his brow knit. "Pillar Doeth, are you okay?"

Slumping, Betsy signaled one of the servers. "A double espresso, please. Cream and sugar."

In a soft whisper, Violet asked, "Can they make it a triple?"

Orson's eyes narrowed. "What did you ask?"

Betsy rubbed her face. "For the last three days, I've been dashing around the planet, answering the emails from people who want to come to our schools and learn magic. I don't want to leave all the work on the shoulders of the four remaining Pillars. I know we can lean a bit on the people of Oz, but ... I don't know. I'm leaving, no one can utilize me, so I just want to do as much as I can."

"Have you gotten any sleep?" Orson sounded concerned, fatherly.

"Yes." She huffed out a small laugh but heard Violet mumble 'no' next to her. "It was just last night. There was this Japanese family. Their daughter was scared of what she was sensing. She felt overwhelmed. That said, they didn't want her to miss any school. They requested someone stop in after four in the afternoon their time. That was two this morning. By the time I got home, it was almost four. I really tried to be as efficient as I could, but I couldn't just transport in and snatch them to Africa. There's always some discussion first. Protocol, especially in places like Japan."

His face tightened. "I understand your desire to maintain your part of the work, Betsy, but couldn't one of the others have done that? Wouldn't it have been simpler for Ania to go?"

"That's what I said!" Violet exclaimed. "And when I mentioned that, Betsy said the others agreed with me." She bumped her shoulder into Betsy to take the bite from her words.

The server placed the drink down next to Betsy's plate, and she sighed when the aroma filled the air around her. After sipping the divine drink, she leaned back. "In theory, I agree with you. The family had seen me on TV at all the different press conferences. In their email, they specifically requested me. I know that they probably would've dealt with any of the Pillars, but I felt that since I was available, I should go."

"But, my friend, will you be able to function today?" His concern warmed her.

She shrugged. "I mean, beyond this brunch and a meeting with the Pillars, I don't have much on my docket for today."

He sipped his tea. "Okay, fair enough. Let's discuss Mr. Hopkins."

"Do we have to? Did he cry to you, tell you I'd been mean to him?"

Orson chuckled. "He did. I explained to him, again, his role. I'll have Ms. Tips create a checklist of duties he should perform before, during, and after each of his meetings with any Pillar, alien, or higher-up. Maybe then there will be fewer of these calls from him."

Betsy clenched her jaw, trying not to react. She could imagine Juk's reaction to having Miranda, a mere executive assistant, directing him on his duties. Personally, she thought the idea was amazing.

Violet finished off her pancakes and reached for some protein. "Will he go through some training, so he isn't so—" her face scrunched up while she thought, "—offensive?"

A small smile played on Orson's face. "That can be arranged. We don't want any of our off-world friends to think us anything but welcoming."

She awarded him with a wide smile before digging in to more of the delicious food.

Betsy's eyes widened when she realized there was a small delicate bowl next to Violet filled with vegemite. *Gods below, I must have been fully dead to have missed that!*

"I had another reason for inviting you here." Orson's voice shook Betsy from her contemplation of the controversial spread. "I was hoping to convince you to bring some of my ... or, our people with you. You know, government people, maybe military guards."

She shook her head, uncertain of what he meant. "Wait, what? Why?"

"Safety, my girl, safety." He leaned back, small mug in hand. "You're not only heading out into the depths of space, you're going out to a possible battle. I'd love to know that we've sent you with the best hope of success possible."

Finishing her coffee, Betsy sent a quick thanks to the kitchen for their amazing brew. She finally felt like she could think. "I really appreciate the thought, however, Thorn is sending a chanzii ship. I can't imagine it won't have a full complement of their military best who are trained for this type of thing." She shot Violet a look.

"Yes, our ships are always fully prepared for anything," she confirmed.

"Our first stop will be Grarrou. If we feel we need more help, we can ask the qynad to lend us some of theirs. They would make better sentries and fighters than just about any of our non-magic wielding allies."

Orson nodded as she spoke. "I see you've thought about this. I'd like more of our own going, but I'll leave the final plans up to you. Make sure to email the final list to me and Juk, as well as, I assume, the other Pillars."

"Of course."

"Betsy, wake up!"

The cloud of warmth seemed to suck her in, and Betsy groaned, turning over and pulling her blanket tighter.

A low laugh wrapped around her, sinking deep. "I know you want to sleep more, but I let you have three hours and now you need to meet with the other Pillars."

Opening her eyes, Betsy gazed over her shoulder at Violet looking beautiful, and awake. *The bitch!*

With a groan, she pushed herself up, letting the cocoon of blankets fall away. "Fine. I'll be ... pleasant."

Violet snorted. "I was hoping for human, but if you think you can achieve something more, go for it!"

Betsy snarled but made it out of bed. She smelled coffee and sighed, deciding Violet was more of a saint than evil. Sipping at the sweetened brew, she felt the power of it strengthen her more than it should. Eyes wide, she gaped at the other woman.

"What? I spoke to Pearl. That soap did wonders the other morning to wake me up ... well, us up. I assume you didn't use it this morning because you woke up late. I went to Oz, got the coffee, creamer, and some quiche, which is by your computer. I figure once you have the full meal you'll be up for a week."

Betsy snorted, sipped her coffee, then headed to the bathroom to make sure she was ready for human interactions.

The online meeting had boxes for each of the Pillars. At one point, Betsy thought Viera would join their ranks, but after falling in love with Thorn, she'd moved to Abritos to become a liaison or an ambassador, whichever word she decided to title herself.

Ania smirked. "I heard about your pick-up in Japan. Did you get any sleep?"

"Some. I can sleep later," she said, finally feeling awake. *I wonder how long this magic will last?*

Zuza shook his head. "I know you felt you needed to do your part, Betsy, but you really didn't have to do so much. We know that you're leaving for an important reason."

The others nodded.

Marco's face had tightened as Zuza spoke. Finally, he leaned forward. "I don't think Betsy should go alone. It's too big a mission."

One of Betsy's brows rose, but Kafi spoke first. "And you think you should go? Is this because you and Pearl have formed a relationship?"

A blush-colored Marco's face. "No, not at all. I just think—"

Ania shook her head. "I disagree." She leaned forward. "And before you ask, no, it isn't because you're young, or because you're in love." Marco's mouth dropped open. "You and Betsy share the same proficiencies. As the saying goes, anything you can do, she can do better."

"Do *you* want to go?" Zuza spoke softly.

"No, my friend. I don't want to leave Sydney any more than you want to leave London." She laughed.

Eyes shut, Zuza shook his head. "You're wrong. I think I'm the perfect second for this trip."

Betsy perked up at that. She and Zuza had traveled together a lot in their youth and did it well. She wouldn't object to either, but she agreed that she and Zuza complemented each other.

There was a moment of silence, then Marco's eyes narrowed. "No. I disagree. I know everyone better. I think I should go."

Kafi nodded. "In this, I agree. Marco knows Pearl. He can support her adjusting to being in space without the magical blanket. He can help after she has her encounter with the krottel, regardless of how that goes. And then—"

"And then what?" Zuza asked, his voice tight. "As was noted, Marco and Betsy share, for the most part, magical proficiencies. In that list, even with Betsy's additional proficiency making her an Elder, neither of you can do the sensing magic I can. Not only can I help if the bugs do to Pearl what they did to Viera, I can also determine which magics she has."

Ania slumped. "If that's the case, should the dwarf go, too, or instead of any of us? The highest probability is that Pearl will have imbuing. If we want her to start training and getting any sort of control, isn't Elder Balzeno our best addition?"

Betsy rubbed her face. "Yes, and we can ask him again, but he seems to want to stay here and work with the new students at magic school."

"It's true." Kafi shrugged. "I can speak to him after the meeting, bring up our new worries, but my guess is, he'll decline."

Marco spoke with someone else in the room with him. Like Betsy, he wasn't alone. It wasn't against any of their rules, but it wasn't usually done.

Betsy, at least, had the decency to pretend she was alone.

The microphone icon indicated it was back on before Marco spoke. "Sorry about that. Pearl is here. She knew this had to do with the trip and she was curious. I should've told you she was in the room. Anyway, she agrees that Zuza would be beneficial, especially if she has sensing as a wild proficiency. She knows it may not happen, but either way, the variety of proficiencies is greater with Zuza than with me." His face tightened as he admitted the truth, hammering in the final nail that would exclude him from the mission.

A smile spread on Zuza's face. "Excellent. Betsy and I haven't traveled the stars together in quite a while. This should be fun."

Despite her worry, Betsy smiled back. She and Zuza always had fun traveling through space together.

A Magical Spark

Betsy

Saturday after breakfast, Betsy felt much better. She had finally gotten sleep and wasn't sure what to do with all her natural energy. As she buzzed around the house, cleaning from a week of barely being home, Violet watched her, snickering.

"You know, we do have plans today."

Wiping down the counter, Betsy narrowed her eyes at the other woman. "We do? Do they involve a bed and fewer clothes?"

Violet snorted. "No, in fact they don't. I have an appointment with Devlin in Africa." She checked her watch. "Actually, it starts soon."

"Okay, so *you* have plans."

Violet threw a spoon at her, nicking her in the arm, and Betsy laughed.

They landed at the magic school just after lunch, local time. They saw the others in the field, and Violet jogged out to meet them. "I don't want to be late for the lesson."

When Betsy got there, she met up with Kafi, who gave her a side hug. "Violet has become his best student. She's been here a few times this week, and her stones are becoming good enough that I think Devlin is moving her up to multiple stones at once. She's getting to the point she can make something close to what the people of Oz use."

Betsy had to work to keep her jaw from dropping. "In her first week? Really?"

Pride filled her as she thought of how amazing her girlfriend was.

"I know, we're all really impressed. She's really taken to gem magic. A natural."

As Violet, and the other students, got down to doing their tasks, Betsy let her third eye, so to speak, watch the magics swirl around them. For some, it was a cloud, with tendrils, almost like a thunderstorm, with flashes of lightning. As the electrical storm hit down, the magic would enter their circle and the destination that they directed it towards.

For Violet, she had something closer to a twister that she wielded like a fine writing utensil. The power gathering above her, ready to do her bidding, and she, the artist, directing exactly how and where she wanted it to go.

As the dance of wild magic and witch continued, Betsy leaned towards Kafi. "Have you watched this in the magical sight?"

"I have. It's like traveling to the Grand Canyon during the end of days and seeing the most extreme weather systems happening all at once. Storms.

Twisters. It gave me shivers. But it's beauty in chaos at the same time."

Betsy nodded. "Yeah, exactly."

Capturing the magic and imbuing it into the gems wasn't a fast process. Some of the lightning escaped the clutches of students, dissipating before being confined into the stones it had been destined to power.

That said, at the end of the lesson, most students looked to be successful.

Eyes dry and head starting to pound, Betsy dropped the magical vision and walked over to where Devlin and Balzeno spoke.

"Do you think it would be possible? I worry the magic would disintegrate the material." Devlin's face tightened as he gazed over the students scattered around the field. Though he spoke to the dwarf, his focus was on his duties.

Balzeno's head tilted, mainly watching Violet and the other students whose skills were the strongest. Like Devlin, it didn't stop him from focusing on their conversation. "You may be right, my boy, but we must try, don't you think? It's the best material for the job. If it doesn't work, we can move on to something else."

"What material?" Betsy asked.

Neither of them had reacted to her approach. After a pause, Devlin sighed. "We've been discussing the issue of cellphones and other electrical devices. Our first thought was to imbue leather for the phones. I just worry the material isn't strong enough to hold the magic."

"Didn't Dulaine imbue all her clothes?" Betsy remembered the explosion. "Or do the different forms of magical imbuing mean it works differently."

"That's true," Devlin said, sounding happier. "Okay, leather. We'll start there. Though, if we do get this to work, we can't go around putting everything we own that's electrical in leather. It would be nice to figure out a way to have a gem or something else 'eat' whatever it is we do that messes up the electricity."

Betsy thought about the problem. It had been plaguing the town since technology had been becoming more and more intricate. She wanted to figure out ways in which the wizards could help. "Have you had one of us watch? We can see the magic moving. Maybe we can help."

Devlin's eyes widened. "You can what now?"

Turning to Balzeno, Betsy tried to hold a neutral face. "You haven't mentioned to him that you can see the magic flowing? That you can tell before the students bring their gems up which ones will be successful and which won't? Or, that you know who the strongest practitioners are?"

The dwarf threw his head back and laughed. Once he got his amusement under control, he shook his head. "No, my dear. I decided to let him run his class his way. He didn't need a doddering old dwarf to interfere. I'm having fun learning his methods."

"Wait, is this magical sight something that can be taught, or is it wizards only?" Devlin sounded hopeful ... desperate even.

"I believe you have to have it on your own. It's an instinct, my boy." Balzeno patted him on the back.

Betsy turned to watch the students as they finished up. "Well, it seems to me, from the students to the electronics, you two will be quite busy while we're away!"

She turned back just in time to see the almost manic looks of excitement on their faces. Her amusement at two such different beings acting so alike brought her real joy.

A New Player In Town

Dulaine

Every morning was the same. The tea sat on the side table, waiting to comfort Dulaine from the coolness in the room. She pushed up, sipped at the tea, and reminded herself of each member of her family and other people from the community of Oz she refused to forget again. She let the tea warm her hands as it helped to wake her up.

I'm going to have to drink coffee or caffeinated tea if ... no, when I get home. This new addiction is another gift from Max'ina and the stupid elves.

Her routine was set. Get up, get out of bed, get ready for the day.

As much as the tuvan excited her, because how could animals that looked like a rainbow of unicorns not make her heart sing, knowing that Max'ina had magicked her for so long had depressed her as well.

Dulaine felt under her pillow for the small stone that kept her mind free, let her remember her home and her family, and made her emotions hers. She knew that meant she wasn't happy all the time, but in the end she preferred to be a bit sad over not remembering who she was and the people she loved.

The small stone secured in her fist, she headed into the closet that led to the bathroom. She selected a black pair of pants and a red top today. She'd match her mount as they dashed around the field. The thought made her smile when very little else did.

In the bathroom, she took her time in the shower. In the beginning, she'd spent little time in this room, not seeing any point. Now she felt it was her safe zone. She knew as soon as she left she'd find Max'ina sitting at the small table with food. They'd eat breakfast together and then head out to the field. Once she left the bathroom, she'd have to pretend to be happy, as if she didn't remember her family and how sad she felt.

Time in the field, out of the house, meant time to stretch. It was nice to leave the room that was little more than a luxury prison.

Once clean and dry, she knew she'd spent as much time as she could justify in that space. If she spent too much time, Max'ina may become suspicious of her motives. She didn't want the elf-woman to wonder about her spell not working.

In the closet, before heading out for breakfast, Dulaine stopped by the door.

Smile on face, you can do this. You are happy, you're about to go out and care for the tuvan, whom you love, and Max'ina is just a way to get out of this room. The food is nourishment, which you need. There is nothing to worry about, save getting off the planet, and that won't happen until you gain the trust of this woman who is acting as your friend. Smile, gain her trust, and maybe she'll tell you about the real threat. Remember, you are nothing but a girl who isn't a burden to anyone at all.

Dulaine didn't know who had taken her, but that was her real worry. She wanted Max'ina's report to be that she was easy to manipulate and hoped all their guards would be down so that her eventual escape would be easier.

She took one last breath, then headed out for breakfast with the elf.

At the table ... sat the wrong elf. She paused, gaping at the person—the elf. He was thinner than Max'ina, and paler, as if he'd never been in the sun and lost his purple tone. *Is that a thing?*

After a moment, she realized she gaped, and forced her mouth shut. Dropping her hand from the closet door, she stood staring at the stranger in her room.

He finally quirked a smile at her. "Hello, child. It is good to finally make your acquaintance."

"Are you the person who stole me away and brought me here?" She couldn't stop the anger in her tone.

His smile grew. "Ah, a bit of backbone to you, good. I like that. Working with spineless pushovers has never been my favorite thing." He waved a hand. "Please, sit. I hear this is your routine. Up, dress, food. I wouldn't want you to become faint with hunger. I've learned that your species can do that."

She wasn't sure he knew as much about humans as he thought, but Dulaine knew that she wanted to eat and a hunger strike would probably only harm her.

On the table was a plate with something that looked like fried potatoes and eggs. She'd had something like this before. It didn't quite taste right, but it was edible.

Across from her, the elf ate the same type of food, too.

Once they'd each finished most of what was on their plates, he leaned back and smiled. "My name is Yav'til. You are correct that I have invited you here. I hope we can be friends."

A small huff of a laugh escaped her before she could stop it. She had hoped to be like Betsy and not show any reaction. "If you invited me here, does that mean I can request to head home? Because, if

I were to be honest, I'm ready. I miss my own bed and the food here is fine, but I miss the food I'm used to."

He nodded, as if in agreement. "That can be arranged, but unfortunately, right now, we don't have any means of getting you there. I was dropped off and don't have a ship. I couldn't get you home until we secure another one. So, while we wait for transportation, can't we at least be civil, if not friends?"

There was something about him ... she wasn't sure. But what he said sounded okay. "Really? You don't have a ship?"

He laughed. "Oh, no. Ships are too easily tracked. Being tracked is the last thing I need or want."

Of all the things he'd said, that at least sounded truthful.

"Since you're here instead of Max'ina, does that mean we won't see the tuvan today? Is she with them without me?"

Yav'til continued to watch her with a pleasant look on his face. "She's around, child. Who do you think cooked this meal?"

He made it sound like he wouldn't dare cook himself. Dulaine was starting to not like him as much. Did he not cook because he didn't know how to, or did he think boys couldn't cook? Again, she worked at keeping her thoughts and emotions from her face.

After a few moments, he continued. "As for us, you'll have some time with the beasts today. Max'ina told me that you've befriended a couple of them. I think that that's great." There was a weird gleam to his eyes. "But, I was thinking, when you were back on your planet, you were being taught magic, right?"

Dulaine slowly nodded. "All my life, but it was only in the last few days that any of it really seemed to stick."

"Excellent. Well, I wouldn't want you to get behind. I happen to be an expert. I was thinking, why don't I continue your lessons?"

A thrill shot through Dulaine at that. "Really? You know magic? What proficiencies?"

"All of them, my child. I am old enough that I can do a little of everything. Though, there are some things I can do quite a lot with. What would you like me to teach you?"

She bit her lip. "I'd really like to get better at imbuing. I've heard it's a lost art and if I could show ... well, show people back home, I think it would be good."

His eyes almost glowed with happiness. *Maybe he likes magic as much as I do.* Then his eyes narrowed. "I believe we can make that work." The smile that stretched across his face caused a chill to slither down Dulaine's back. "Then we have a plan. You can spend some time with the tuvan, but not too much, they're just beastly diversions from this planet. What we'll really focus on while we wait for a new ship to arrive to take you home is learning magic."

A wide smile spread on Dulaine's face as excitement surged through her and she shimmied in her seat.

Yav'til leaned in. "One question, child."

She paused, eyes widening. "What?" Her voice had gotten quieter with his sudden approach.

"Did you know that our whole conversation has been in the elvish language? The language of magic?"

Shock slammed into Dulaine. "But ... what? I only know English. That's not possible."

"But it is, child. And when you spoke with Max'ina, you spoke Galactic Standard. You know several languages, child, not just the one."

13

The Future

Betsy

Sunday morning, Betsy woke up before the sun ... or Violet. She slipped from bed and headed down to make breakfast. Though the panel could create a great meal, she sometimes enjoyed cooking.

Over the last few months, things had been hectic and there hadn't been time to spend in the kitchen relaxing and preparing breakfast. *I bet Violet would enjoy a last meal, so to speak. There may be a few more before we leave, but one I make may be more meaningful.*

Betsy paused, thinking about that and about how much Violet had grown to mean to her. She realized once again, she enjoyed sharing space with someone besides the ven.

Maybe I'll ask her to move in with me when we get back.

As the idea dug in deep and warmth filled her, another part of her mind snickered. *Maybe I should ask her to be more than just my roommate and bedmate.*

The enormity hit her. She'd lived for years, centuries, and she'd never thought of having someone in her life permanently. *But I love her ... and I want her with me, always.*

A smile stretched across her face as she got out the ingredients and made bread pudding, sausage, eggs, and hash browns. It got so wide, her cheeks hurt. With a snort, Betsy ordered up a coffee from the panel. It was easier and nicer than trying to have one more machine on her counter.

As she plated the meal, Violet came into the kitchen. "You didn't wake me up! And what's the smile about? You don't look trustworthy."

The smile widened and Betsy wondered if her cheeks would ever be the same. *I didn't think it could get bigger.* "I'm fine, it's fine. Everything's fine. I just thought I'd let you sleep, Major. I figure the ship's due any day now and you'll be on that bridge every morning for weeks. You may not get a late morning again." Betsy pulled Violet in, hands on her hips, so they were touching. "Is it okay that I cooked for you?" She raised one eyebrow then leaned in for a kiss. She suddenly felt giddy, like a kid in a candy store.

Violet yawned and smiled back, though not as wide. "It's fine," she looked confused, "but I like watching you cook, and I won't be able to do that again for weeks. And then, who knows. We'll both be back and busy trying to catch up on over a month of work."

Betsy smiled. "Well, we'll just have to make cooking a priority, won't we?"

"Yes. Once we get things settled down and have time."

"Hmm." Betsy pulled Violet back in for an embrace, swaying slightly from her extra energy. "You know. If you moved in here with me and the ven we would have a lot more opportunity for cooking together."

Violet froze, pausing Betsy's movement as well. "What did you say? Because I haven't had coffee and am still very tired, but it sounded like you asked me to move into your high-tech private home with all its traps and do not enter spells."

Tightening the hug, Betsy dipped down for another kiss, losing herself in the feel and taste of the other woman. Once they separated, she rested her forehead on Violet's. "Okay, order up a couple of coffees, I need more, so that you can answer with a clear mind."

They sat at the table. Violet sipped her coffee, then narrowed her eyes. "Are you sure you want me to move in here? Like, full-time?"

Just hearing the words sent shivers of joy throughout Betsy. She never thought she'd feel this way about having another person in her domain. "Yes. I do. I want to spend as much of my free time with you as I can. I love you Violet. I never thought

I'd feel such a connection with anyone else, but yes, please move in with me."

As Betsy spoke, Violet's face brightened. When she finished, Violet leapt up to give her a hug and another searing kiss. "Let's survive this trip, whenever we finally get to leave, before we make any big decisions, but yes, I love the idea of sleeping next to you every night, waking up next to you every morning, and spending all the free time I have annoying you."

A laugh erupted from Betsy. "Sit, you fool! We need to eat, and the food isn't improving as we talk."

They both dug in.

Violet leaned back, sipping her coffee. "Okay, we have today off. No more globe-trotting. No magic lessons. No meetings. What do you want to do?"

"Have you checked email? Has your fearless chanzii leader sent anything? Do we have an ETA for the ship?"

Violet's lip twitched. "You know, if I don't check email, then I can ignore my duties for the day, and we can just pretend to have a completely free day."

"That is, until a ship shows up expecting you to lead them." Both Betsy's eyebrows rose in challenge.

With a grunt, Violet glared at her. "Fine, but if the ship shows up today, and my day of leisure is ruined, I'm blaming you."

Betsy laughed. "You know that makes no sense, right?"

"If I don't check, I'm pretty sure it can't show up until at least Tuesday. That's how it works." Violet smiled, eyes dancing.

"In what universe?"

"Mine? I mean, it *should* work that way. It always shows up one day after I check."

Betsy rubbed her face. "So, you're saying, if you check now, it'll show up tomorrow, and our day of nothing will turn into a day of packing and final preparations?"

"That is what I'm saying." Violet held her hand out, phone waving between them. "So, what's your final decision, Elder? Do we have a day to ourselves to celebrate our newest almost decision, or do we ruin it by checking the status of the ship?"

Betsy barked a laugh. "That is ridiculous, you know that, right? The ship is on its way here. It's been on its way since it left Abritos. Nothing we do now will affect its arrival."

"So, choose."

"Just check your email." Betsy shook her head, then finished her breakfast.

Violet glared. "Just remember, this will all be your fault. You'll owe me big!"

Betsy laughed as she started clearing off the table.

"Gah! I told you. I totally told you so! I knew it! Why didn't you believe me? I was right."

Dishes in the sink, Betsy took a towel and wiped down the table before she started washing everything. "So, you're saying the ship arrives tomorrow?"

"Yes! That's what I'm saying. It's always the day after I look."

"So, why didn't you wait until tomorrow to look?" Betsy gave her a wide-eyed stare; glad the table was clear of anything Violet could throw.

After Betsy sent messages off to Orson and Juk informing them of their departure plans, she called Zuza to let him know he should pack. He said he'd update the other Pillars and Pearl. Lastly, Betsy contacted Xantay, who was excited for the trip. She said her backup would happily cover for her while she was away.

Betsy had done some packing all week, so the process wasn't as bad as Violet had made it out to be. They decided to bring everything to the Athletic Center in the chanzii part of town. It was a safe place to convey their luggage, and a one-stop transport the ships all knew. Because of that, Betsy intended on staying with Violet.

As for the ven, she planned on leaving them at magic school. Kafi agreed to watch them, and they'd have a lot of space to fly and have fun. Ania also volunteered to have them at her place, but Betsy worried she may not get them back if Ania got her hands on her companions. There really wasn't any lack of volunteers to watch the pets. Everyone loved them.

On Monday, the group leaving to get Dulaine met at the Athletic Center. A few others joined to see them off—Pearl's parents, Marco, Devlin, and Balzeno.

Juniper had brought the ship. It was a similar size to the Ziner, but that one hadn't been available.

"Ensign Snow to Major North. Ship Hoftil, here for transfer." Juniper's voice came over clear and excited.

"Major North, ready for transport." Most of the crowd spoke in small groups and didn't see when Violet disappeared, heading up first to check over the ship she was about to lead.

Despite this being something Betsy had done in the past, tendrils of nerves danced throughout her body as she gazed around the room.

This is it, the last few minutes before we head off to fight for the life of a child.

14

And Away We Go

Betsy

There were a lot of beings milling about the Athletic Center. Betsy wasn't even sure anyone had noticed Violet leave. It would take her a few minutes to do a walk-through of the ship—what had Juniper said? The Hoftil?—and then Violet would begin bringing the rest of the passengers up.

Stepping back, she leaned against the wall by the luggage, watching the others as they prepared for the trip. She decided to take a moment to take in the calm before the storm. She figured there wouldn't be much time to relax in the next few weeks.

Near the center, Pearl stood with her people. Her parents had wide smiles and kept hugging her. Marco had a hand on the small of her back, his face tight. *I wonder if he's hiding worry for Pearl, anger at not being able to join us, or a combination of both.*

Most of the bags for the people traveling were piled near Betsy, but there were a few bags in Pearl's parents' hands. I wonder what they've sent along. *That town ... they are always up to something.* She chuckled, thinking about their shenanigans.

Devlin and Balzeno stood with Xantay at the far end. Xantay bounced with animation over whatever story she was telling. Devlin's smile couldn't get any bigger. *I wonder how long he'll fanboy over dragons, what he thought were mythical beasts, and the new magics, and everything else he doesn't know.* She laughed at his enjoyment.

After a few minutes of taking everything in, Betsy headed over to the trio. "Morning, all. Balzeno, change your mind? Coming with us?"

The dwarf smirked. "Betsy, good to see you this morning. And no, you'll do better without me. I have too much history with Yav'til. I'm sure he's up to no good. If I'm there, it'll be about capture and punishment. He's been, as you say here, on the lamb for centuries. If it's just you and the chanzii, beings that have no history with him, things will run more smoothly."

Betsy sighed. "I understand, but part of me believes having you would benefit us."

"I have things to do here, Elder. You'll have to be the leader on the trip." His brows waggled.

Betsy crossed her arms. "You think I wouldn't have been anyway?" She winked at him. "That's cute. But, that said, we'll miss you."

Devlin snickered. "You two are hilarious. As for me, I'm glad Elder Balzeno is staying. We have a project, and though I know it could easily be put off a month or so, I don't want to wait."

Both Balzeno and Xantay laughed. The image of three different aliens discussing a project so calmly fulfilled something within Betsy she hadn't realized she needed filled. It brought joy to watch their byplay.

Before they could speak more, the door opened and Juk walked in. It took a moment for Betsy to work her face into a neutral mask. She hadn't expected to see him again before her return.

His head swung back and forth, taking in everyone in the room, before he walked across to Betsy.

With each step he took, her jaw tightened. Once she realized what she was doing, she forced herself to relax. She didn't want to start the trip with a migraine.

He stopped a few feet away. "Betsy."

Balzeno's voice grumbled out, deeper than normal. "That's Elder Doeth, youngling. Show proper respect when speaking in a public forum."

His eyes darted between Betsy and the dwarf and back before he licked his lips. "Right, okay. Elder Doeth." He took a breath. "I wanted to officially send you off. I knew you were leaving today and wanted to make sure the department had a showing."

"Okay." Betsy narrowed her eyes, gazing at him. "You've shown up, we acknowledge you, and you can leave."

He cleared his throat. "Right, but, I also wanted to offer to ... um, if you wanted, I could join you."

The room got quiet. Apparently even the other group had been listening in. Betsy blew out a breath. "Whereas I appreciate the offer, I know how *busy* you are, and how *full* your schedule always is. I can't imagine you taking off an entire month, if not more."

His face tightened. "Right, busy. What about taking some of our troops, some security? We ... I would hate for you to go and be endangered, knowing you could have brought help."

Betsy took a moment to center herself before responding. "Are you here on your own, or did Orson send you? I already spoke to Orson about this. The chanzii sent a ship to rescue Dulaine. The ship is fully staffed, including with some of their military. Our people aren't qualified for galactic travel, much less battle. Leave this for the chanzii, beings who are trained, like I told your boss."

Juk stood, gazing at Betsy, disappointment oozing from him. "So, you don't want me or any of our troops. You're doing this without any governmental oversight or inclusion."

"Yes. In a way. You do know that I was one of the founders of the governmental department you currently work for. I've told you this. Orson has told you this. It is in the documentation. By being on this mission, the government is naturally there ... or at least the department is being represented." Betsy tried to keep her voice from rising or speeding up, but the number of times Juk had pissed her off was getting unbearable.

Marco walked up and put a hand on Juk's shoulder. "If it helps, I'm not invited either." His voice was steady. More mature than Betsy thought Juk would ever achieve. "I know I haven't had many meetings with you, but I could take over for the next few weeks and keep you up to date on what's going on. I know that you enjoy your weekly updates with Betsy, but she'll be gone, and I'll be here."

Juk's eyes widened a bit and his mouth gaped. Then he shook his head, as if trying to clear his thoughts. "Yeah, that would be great. I was worried I'd have to—I mean the department would have to— go blind for the duration of Betsy's absence. If you wouldn't mind, I'd really appreciate it."

Betsy nearly fell over at the fawning and respect Juk gave Marco. Was it because he didn't know the other Pillar or was it a sexist thing? She decided she'd figure it out when she returned. Maybe she'd let Marco take over as the permanent point-person for a while. She'd been doing it long enough. She could work with the aliens, he could work with the government.

"Elder Doeth, it's Ensign Snow on the Hoftil. We can begin transporting people up."

A small squeal came from Pearl.

Porter handed her a bag. "Don't forget the town's gifts. Store them well and make sure to use them as needed. We want you and your sister to make it home."

Pearl gave both her parents and Marco a hug.

"Ensign Snow, I think we're ready. Why don't you start with Pearl and Zuza."

Next to her, Balzeno shook his head. "I need to speak with him for a moment, if you don't mind."

"Scratch that, Juniper. Start with Xantay and Pearl. Then take me. Zuza will let you know when he's ready."

Pearl ran over to give Devlin a hug before she was transported away.

Devlin walked over to Betsy. "I have a gift for Violet. I was going to give it to her before she left. I didn't know she was going to be transported so quickly."

Betsy laughed. "Yeah, the captain of the ship has to be the first up to meet the crew and check everything over. Once she's settled, then we can go."

Devlin's eyes widened. "When did the luggage transport away?"

Betsy looked over her shoulder to where she'd been standing with the bags. The space was now empty. "Probably when we were distracted by Juk." She faced the young man again. "Stay safe and have fun teaching." She gave him a hug. He appeared shocked for a moment, then returned the gesture. Afterwards he handed her a box with a handle.

Balzeno came over to them. "Elder Doeth, safe travels. I know you will do well and return with our young Dulaine."

A warmth filled her at his words. She felt confident in her ability to get Dulaine home, even in the face of an old scary elf, but having Elder Balzeno's belief in her as well meant something.

Vicki and Porter were the last to come over and wish her well, each giving her the kind of hug only a parent can give.

The world shimmered around her like a watercolor painting being washed away. Then Betsy was on the transport pad of a spaceship. In front of her was Juniper and Pearl. The first had a huge smile, the second looked excited and terrified.

15

*A Whole New Not-World …
But Something*

Pearl

Betsy appeared on the pad. "I take it Xantay already left to get to the bridge to help out?"

The other person ... being? She was turquoise with purple hair ... said something. Betsy nodded with a smile. Then the being waved at first

Pearl, then Betsy, then back, her eyes warm and inviting.

Embarrassed at not understanding what was going on, Pearl fisted her hands, then looked down at them. *What did I do? Damn it. I've gotten lazy. Everyone on Earth speaks English. Even Xantay has been using the gem. I haven't had to use my translator for so long, I totally forgot it in the quick packing to get here.*

Pearl finally gazed up when she realized the room had gone silent. Betsy said, "Pearl, are you okay?"

"What? Oh, right, yeah, I'm fine. Why?"

"Ensign Snow suggested I take you to your room then give you a tour. She said she'd spoken to you but then saw you weren't wearing a translator." Betsy looked amused. "I take it you forgot it."

Pearl slumped. "Everything in the last two days just happened so quickly. I swear the thing was on top of my suitcase ... I don't know."

"Don't worry, we can pick you up a new one. They have plenty on board. And for now, I can show you around. The people you'll be spending the majority of your time with speak English." Betsy waved at their bags. "Let's go."

The ship was big, larger than Pearl remembered from the Ziner. When she was on that vessel she was half in shock at being on a spaceship and in the intervening time she thought her memories had expanded all her impressions. They hadn't. The hallways—corridors?—were spacious—huge!—with black paneling. "I didn't expect it to be so ... I don't know what I thought."

"It's a lot. Just remember, the space has to be large enough for the qynads. They tend to want to be able to walk next to each other."

What an idiot! Pearl could slap herself silly. "Why didn't I think of that?"

"Probably because you've had a lot of other things to think about." Betsy stopped. "Okay, first rule. We're in space, you'll see that soon enough. Nothing we're about to do is in your wheelhouse of knowledge. You can't beat yourself up every time something happens you're not used to or comfortable with. Just get into the mindset that everything will be different, odd, and unexpected. Then you'll be ready for nothing. It's a good starting place."

Pearl laughed. "Got it. Be ready for nothing. Check."

"Now, you've seen these panels before, right?"

"I have, but I didn't realize anything black and shiny would be a computer panel." Pearl's hand lifted to touch the panel then dropped.

"It's okay, you can touch it. It also understands English. Let's start with this: tap the panel and ask it where your room is. Get used to interacting with the computer."

Excited at the idea, Pearl touched the panel and it lit up. "Um, hi, panel. It's Pearl ... um, Pearl Katz. Can you tell me where my room is?"

Instead of speaking to her, lights lit a path on the panel and along the side of the floor in a cascade from her feet in the direction she should go, repeating the pattern. "Oh! That's great. I can just follow the way the lights direct me."

The two continued. When they got to a longer corridor, Pearl eyed Betsy. "Did you know where to go without the lights?"

"I did. This ship is the same model as the Ziner, and I've been on that one a lot. I was assigned accommodations close to the one I usually get, and yours is near mine. After I show you the area and the amenities, I'll give you the grand tour."

"Is there much to see? Like, is it more than a bedroom, a place to eat, and a center for driving the ship?" Pearl's brow knit. "A bridge, right?"

"Yes, they navigate from the bridge. And there are several other locations. Training rooms. If you end up getting magic, we'll use those spots quite a bit. There are also exercise rooms that help for both health and boredom. There are a few other hotspots: engineering, sick bay, things like that. It's good to know the basic layout."

The lights got them to a lift. Pearl just gaped. "I know how to use an elevator, but this doesn't make any sense."

"No, it wouldn't. The characters are all in Galactic Standard. It was an interesting choice to do that versus their native tongue."

"Why did they?"

"I don't know for certain, but my guess is, when they started to travel into space, they knew they were more of a 'homebody' type of species. Because of that, they'd have other aliens on board helping with different aspects of the day-to-day running of the ship. Using a universal language makes more sense. If you know that you won't have others on board, then you stick with your own language."

"That's right." Pearl nodded. "The krottel forced them to leave. Yet, we're going to ask them for a favor. It's all rather complicated, isn't it?"

"A bit, but I'm hoping it'll all work out in the end."

They got onto the lift and Pearl watched as Betsy tapped some buttons. "How many languages do you speak?"

Betsy shrugged. "English, German, French, Japanese, Galactic Standard, Chanziian, I don't know, a few others. I've had to learn them over the years to make life easier. I do have the translator so I don't need to know all languages but understanding them can be beneficial."

Pearl sighed. "We don't have time during this trip for me to learn anything."

"No, but you're studying a lot and experiencing even more by coming along."

They got to a locked door, and Betsy showed Pearl how to signal to someone inside that you wanted to come in, unlock the entrance of her chamber, and open and lock the door from inside.

The accommodations themselves had two areas, the bed and closet and a washroom.

The main room also had a small desk with a chair. There was a small window that looked out to ... space. Pearl gasped, dropped all of her bags but the one her dad had handed her, and ran to press her nose to the window. It was surprisingly warm. She could see the sun, larger than when on Earth. Besides that, everything was inky dark and dotted with white stars and planets.

It took her breath away.

"I need to show you how to use the shower. You'll need to soak at least twice a day, if not three times." Betsy's voice reminded her there were things to do.

She pulled herself away from the view and followed the other woman into the smaller room. "I know how to shower, Betsy, I've been doing it my whole life ... and what do you mean soak? You don't soak in a shower."

A laugh bubbled out of Betsy. *Is she laughing more than she did when I met her? Is she more relaxed? Happier? I wonder if I'm just imagining things.*

"The showers on the ship don't use water. They have a different technology."

"Wait, what? But I brought some of the soaps and shampoos from town. They created something to help with my not being in the blanket of magic." When she thought about it, she realized she already felt the effects.

"I know, but being up here is different." Betsy's gaze shifted to the bag Pearl still held from her Dad. "Is that what Porter gave you?"

"Yeah, I mean, there are other things besides the shower items, but I was looking forward to something relaxing and familiar."

"Okay, let me show you how the shower works. Again, two or three times a day for you." Pearl watched as Betsy explained there was the button for cleaning, but also one for a magical soak. "You should soak in the morning and at night. If that isn't enough, do one midday as well. You being a witch is something completely new. I don't know how hard all of this will be on you."

"I was also given lotion and some hard candies. I'll be using those as well."

Betsy's eyes narrowed. "I'm curious about all of this. If it helps, I'd like to try anything you are willing to share. Not right now. I'm feeling great. But give me a few days."

Pearl snickered. She didn't know what it would feel like, but she could imagine.

The tour continued after they dropped off Betsy's bags.

"This is the cafeteria."

Pearl froze, then her body trembled. She'd met several aliens around her town and in magic school, but this was like her time on the Ziner. The vast number in this room made her mind hurt. She and Betsy were the only two Earthlings. The rest of the beings that were even close to looking like her had turquoise to blue skin and various shades of purple hair. There were dragons and beings that looked like Bigfoot. There was even one animal that looked like a large cat.

She swallowed. "Okay, um, got it." Pearl backed away until she couldn't see any of the beings in the cafeteria.

"Are you okay?" Zuza came from down the hall. He gazed into the room. "Ah. No, you're not. You do know that none of the beings in there will harm you."

Her head bobbed up and down quickly, mostly without her thought. "It's just ..."

His warm hands rubbed up and down her arms. "You're overwhelmed. Why don't we head back to your room? You, me, and Betsy. I know you're feeling a lot right now."

Her breathing was starting to calm. She hadn't realized how choppy it'd become. "Okay."

Back at her room, she sat on the bed. Betsy sat next to her. Zuza took the desk chair. He smiled, his blue eyes warm. "I know that this is all a lot. Before coming up here, Balzeno suggested you use his language box on the trip to Grarrou to learn Galactic Standard. That way you won't be as affected by the lack of magic and, when you get there, you'll know the language."

Betsy's brow furrowed. "Do we have a box?"

Zuza chuckled. "He did and Juniper transported it to a training room. I guess he sent her instructions on its use. She is smart, very smart. She'll have the workings of that thing down in no time. Anyway, if you're interested, you can be set up in the box in about twenty minutes. Then, next thing you know, we'll be at the qynad planet, and you'll be bilingual."

Betsy nodded. "That's ... wow. I like that. That's what Viera did to learn both Galactic Standard and chanziian."

Pearl hesitated. "Isn't that ... I don't know, cheating."

"In what way?" Zuza's face scrunched up as he looked at her.

"I don't know. I'm cheating in that I'm avoiding acclimating to being around aliens, in learning a language the hard way, in figuring out how to deal with not being in a magical blanket. I guess, all of it."

"No." Both of the Pillars said it at the same time. Betsy continued. "Experiences are not only good if they are hard. Learning the language and avoiding something that could be painful, to me, is a double win. Take Balzeno, one of the smartest beings I know, up on his offer."

Pearl thought about it for another few moments, then nodded. "Okay, fine. Good. I like this plan."

The three headed to the bridge to speak with Violet. She agreed with their plan. After getting the approval, Pearl followed the others to the training room where they met Ensign Snow. She smiled and waved at the box.

The box was black and about the size of a small bed. Inside there was bedding and a pillow. Shivers raced throughout Pearl, making her tremble. It wasn't that she thought anyone was out to get her, but a box that would cause her to sleep for an extended time ... it made her nervous.

It's like surgery. I'll just be out for a few seconds, then everything will be okay.

Betsy patted her back. "I know it seems odd, but you'll be okay. We'll be monitoring you the whole time. I promise."

Her words relaxed Pearl. Betsy would make sure she came out of it healthy on the other side. Betsy was an Elder now.

With a final breath, Pearl stepped in, lay down, and let them put the cover on.

Everything became dark, as inky black as when she looked out the window in her room.

Maybe I should've stayed in my chamber. A hissing sound came from above. *I could've spent each night counting the stars. It would've been amazing, watching how the sky changed as we traveled the galaxy.*

The thought of missing the trip, not seeing each step of the journey from Earth to ... well, wherever Dulaine was, suddenly Pearl knew she had to get out of the box.

For a moment, her eyes shut. Her muscles relaxed.

No! She shook herself. *I need to know where we are. I should keep a journal ... for my sister. She would want to know ... wouldn't she?*

Pearl debated knocking on the side of the box to let the others know she'd changed her mind, but every part of her was heavy.

I can't move. Am I okay?

Her eyes shut again.

I'll just rest my eyes for a minute.

No! I have to be aware for Dulaine.

The box opened. *Did something happen? Did it not work? What went wrong?*

"Hi, Pearl. How do you feel?" Pearl shut her eyes against the bright light. She didn't recognize the voice, but she felt off and wasn't sure she'd recognize her own voice.

"I feel heavy, but okay." Her words were sloppy. She squeezed her eyes tighter and scrunched her face. "I don't think this is going to work."

There was a soft laugh. "No? Why not?"

"I think I should spend my time tracking what we're doing ... you know, for Dulaine. Keep a journal." Pearl finally got her arms working and rubbed her face. "Why am I so stiff? I've only been in here for like—"

"Ten days."

"What? That's not possible. I lay down, thought about what I was doing, decided to change my mind, and then ... what?"

A hand appeared. "Let me help you up. Facing these lights probably isn't helping."

Once Pearl was sitting, she saw she was speaking to the Ensign. "Wait, you don't speak English. How are we talking?"

"Well, my friend, you aren't speaking English."

That woke her up. It felt like a bucket of ice was tossed over her. "I'm ... what?"

"Come on, let's get you food. The box is set to give you nutrition, but I'm sure coffee and something you can chew would probably be even better."

A grumble from Pearl's stomach told her that it was in complete agreement. It took a few moments for Pearl to get herself out of the box. She felt a bit wobbly, but Ensign Snow helped. "Thank you, Ensign Snow."

The other woman laughed. "Gods, call me Juniper."

Pearl felt lighter. "Okay, Juniper." She took a step and started to feel stronger. "I think coffee sounds great."

The two walked to the cafeteria. Just before they got there, Pearl froze. "Last time I was here ..."

"Don't worry, it isn't a mealtime. It won't be as busy."

The room wasn't empty, but there were plenty of places to sit. The table had a panel set down the center. Playing around with the menu, Pearl decided on something that seemed to be a type of oatmeal and coffee.

Juniper nodded. "I'll go get the food. You don't know the ins and outs yet."

Once they started eating, Pearl relaxed. "So, are we at the dragon ... I mean, qynad planet?"

"Yes, we just arrived at Grarrou. Xantay, Betsy, and Violet headed down to speak with the leaders. We're hoping a group of us can travel down later."

"What about Zuza?" Pearl wasn't sure about the seniority amongst the Pillars, but she thought Zuza was older.

"Oh, he was monitoring you last, so he's sleeping. He'll be up soon." Juniper sipped her coffee, gazed into the mug, then sighed. "Do you need a refill, too?"

"Um," Pearl finished the last sip of her coffee and nodded. "Yeah, I could use more."

The Ensign hopped up and went to refill both their mugs. *Wow, she has energy.*

Once they were done with breakfast, Juniper led Pearl to her room. She showered, making sure to do a magical soak, and dressed. Then, finding a notebook in her bag, she began to write a journal of what had happened so far. Because of the box, it was a rather short entry.

A chime let her know she had a visitor.

Zuza stood in the hall. "Hi, Pearl. How are you feeling?"

"Good. Juniper, er, Ensign Snow took me to breakfast."

He nodded. "Great. Well, if you're up to it, it's time to go down to the planet." He held out an earpiece, so she'd be able to communicate with the qynads.

A thrill shot through her, followed by apprehension. Despite her worry, she slipped the earpiece on. "Okay, yes, let's go."

A smile crossed his face as if he followed her jumble of emotions. She narrowed her eyes. "One of your proficiencies is sensing, right?"

"That it is."

"So you do understand when my emotions are like a roller coaster?"

This time he laughed and held out his elbow. "Shall we?"

She hooked her arm in his. "Sounds great."

Pearl thought she was ready to meet dragons. They were majestic and proper and slightly scary. What she hadn't expected was a group in the valley of a mountain to act like a family, a community. They reminded her of what she'd read about hippies with the adults and larger dragons along the edge, in pairs or larger groups, sunning, socializing, or debating and the smaller dragons causing mayhem in the flat of the valley, like any group of toddlers and teens.

At first, Pearl gaped, unsure what to think. Then she laughed, all her tension from the last ... she had no idea how long, released at the antics of kids, no matter the species, acting like kids.

She and Juniper headed down to the valley. It was enormous. They found Xantay with the largest of the youth.

She trotted over. "Juniper, Pearl, these are some of my friends. They are almost old enough to start shadowing adults in their day-to-day work. Isn't that exciting?"

Pearl watched. "So, during the day, do the young just romp around and play?"

One of the qynads with Xantay, an orange beast with yellow wings and red tips, harrumphed. *I wonder if its personality is as fiery as its appearance.* "We have lessons, biped. We learn." She—it sounded feminine—raised her nose a bit higher. "Not only do we have our schooling, needing to master all the things *you* need to master, we have to learn to fly, control our fire, and move around in areas you bipeds think big enough for us. Our schooling is *much* harder. All you two-legs are so arrogant."

There was no way Pearl would either be offended or get in a fight with a qynad, especially on their turf. She just smiled. "Sounds like you've done a lot in your life."

The very fiery qynad's eyes narrowed. "I have. Probably more than *you*."

"Of that, I'm sure." Pearl nodded.

Xantay snorted. "Rastay, you don't have to be rude. If you want off-planet, you'll have to learn to be pleasant. You know that."

"Well, maybe I don't. Interacting with beings who are so ... fragile, and ignorant ... I don't know that it's worth it."

The other qynad, green with black tipped scales, snorted. "Rastay learned she's slated to work here, in the lab. She was tested and unless she goes through testing again, she won't be in a position that interacts with any but other qynads."

Xantay's full body shook. "Whoa. What about you?"

The green qynad bounced. "I passed for intergalactic work."

"Rock on Forrixity. Maybe we'll work together."

A twinkle came from the green dragon's eyes. "I hope so. I'd love to travel."

Rastay grunted and walked off. A gaggle of small dragons flew by, tumbling in the sky. Rastay snarled, "Careful, we have guests and they're delicate." Then she flew away.

Xantay bowed her head. "Pearl, Juniper, this is my friend Forrixity. Forrixity, this is Ensign Snow, um, Miss Katz, this is Forrixity."

Juniper shook her head. "Please call me Juniper."

Pearl felt giddy. "And call me Pearl. It's a pleasure to meet you, Forrixity." She bowed her head. "Can you tell me, what will be your next steps for training? Will you be like Xantay? Do you want to work on a ship?"

The green qynad grunted. "I hope not. One of the adults works on Zy'Boon Space Station Number Four. I'm hoping to intern with him. He's one of their top engineers. If all goes well, I could be an engineer on any one of the space stations."

Pearl had only heard of Torville Station Number Six. "How many space stations are there?"

"Oh, well the Torville family has eight, the Q'olrit family has ten, and the Zy'Boon's have eleven, so twenty-nine. The Q'olrit space stations are pretty far out in the galaxy and aren't as well run. But I'd take anything as long as I can play with electronics."

Xantay shook her head. "There are space stations run by other families, but we just won't travel to them or work for the families. They aren't safe."

Forrixity's tail twitched. "I just don't think about the ones I won't go to. Why mention the unmentionable?"

Before they could argue more, Zuza approached. "Pearl, we've set up a meeting with you and—" He stopped, gazing around at Forrixity and the younger qynads. "We have a meeting and we'd like you to join us."

After saying goodbye to her new ... well, she hoped the qynad could be a friend, she just wasn't sure how things worked with the qynads, she followed Zuza to a pad, and they transported to a cave. It wasn't large, maybe the size of the average living room, and a bed was set up in the center. A being stood to one side. They wore a cape and a mask covered their face.

Zuza nodded. "Thank you for being willing to hear our request."

The—being? Weren't they here to meet a bug?—nodded. "We will speak to you, Pillar of Earth. Then we will go back to our dwelling below the ground."

"When you came to our planet, you revealed to our people the existence of both magic and aliens—"

"And we have been and are paying for that."

Zuza's voice tightened. "You are paying by getting what you wanted. A place to live in peace, with magic you can survive off of. Do not think for a minute I do not understand the true outcome of that meeting, krottel queen."

"We are separated from the rest of our kind—"

"And alive after the atrocities you committed," he snapped out.

There was a silence, heavy and thick. Then Zuza nodded. "We come with a simple request. It will not be one we plan on repeating. It is a direct consequence of what you did."

"Explain."

"Yav'til—"

"We know of him and what he did. Go on." The being waved a hand.

"We believe he wants to start his trials over. He has kidnapped one of the humans from our planet. It is because it became known that our planet had magic users that could imbue that he came at all."

"That isn't our problem." They started to back up.

"Then I'll ask that the qynads rescind their invitation and you'll be ejected to space."

"You can't do that," they screamed, hurting Pearl's ears.

"Oh, you are wrong, krottel queen, I can. Hear the sincerity of my words."

The krottel snapped out words like daggers. "What do you want?"

"I want you to open up the magic in this one." He pointed at Pearl. "In the same way you did to Viera, the human you bit on Torville Station Number Six."

There was a sound. *Is it laughing?* "Why didn't you start with that, human? That is not hard. That isn't a request. We feed from her magic and give back a push. We get more than she gains. Hold out a hand, boy."

"Girl," Pearl mumbled as she did as it bade.

An iridescent bug scuttled to her hand and up her arm. A shiver of revulsion rocketed through her body.

"Brace yourself, human. Or lie on the bed. It will be ... odd, if the other human is any indication. And after the bite, we will leave."

Pearl sat, then she felt a pain, as her memories played behind her eyes like a fast action movie.

She hadn't realized she'd closed her eyes until she opened them. A wave of concern hit her like a mallet. She wrapped her arms around herself. "What am I feeling? What is that? Is that your emotion?"

It suddenly stopped, like water being turned off, and she gasped.

Zuza nodded, then tapped something. "Hoftil, please transport us directly to Pearl's rooms. She needs to rest."

The caves melted away as easily as the fear grew in her gut.

A Lifetime Of Lessons Isn't All It's Cracked Up To Be

Betsy

The sun beat down on the side of the mountain where Betsy sat with a few of the ancient qynads. There were a few large beasts lazing about like huge cats. Several slept, but two sat telling stories of their long lives.

"And then, when the pups flew over the ridge, they thought they were going to fly towards the woods, but all they found was an ocean." He chuckled deep in his belly. "The coos and whoops filled the air. A full rainbow of colors swirled all around us before the lot of them dove into the sea. They splashed in, causing a cascade of eruptions of water. Me and the other monitors roared in laughter at their antics."

Betsy laughed. "All that time, they thought they were on a mission to find a forest? All that complaining? And they ended up in the ocean. That's fantastic!"

"It's a rite of passage. We take them every four to five years, depending on how many young we have."

Leaning back on her elbows, Betsy let the heat of the day soak into her. "And the older pups never let on to the hatchlings?"

One of the other qynads snickered. "They wouldn't dare. Let on to the end goal? They live to hear about how awful the trek was."

"And none of the groups have ever figured it out?" It boggled her mind. This expedition that the qynads did to trick their youth into critical thinking.

"Once or twice a century we get a cluster with a hatchling that critically thinks about the clues. It's a thrill for the adults."

Before Betsy could get more of this story, her radio went off. "Elder Doeth, Pillar Brzezinski has requested your presence on the ship. Can we transport you?"

She nodded with respect at the qynad, stood, then tapped her communicator. "Yes, I'm ready."

The qynads all tilted their heads to her as they melted into a multicolored swirl of colors. The elders on the hill. The hatchlings flying in the sky behind them. The youth running amok in the field below. *I really need to return and spend more time here. They are such a welcoming group.*

Betsy expected to land on the platform on the Hoftil, face to face with Juniper, or one of her people. Instead, she stood in Pearl's room. The adolescent herself lay on her bed, Zuza sitting next to her.

"Did it work? Is she okay?" Worry slammed into her. She hadn't seen Viera after the krottel had opened up her magic. How hard of a transition had it been?

Pearl grunted. "I'm fine, stop worrying."

Betsy sighed, gazing at her.

Both Pearl and Zuza slowly turned to face her. Pearl's hands covered her face. "Please, just ... I'm fine."

Zuza smiled. "As they did with Pillar Kor, our young Pearl was given an extra gift. I fear she may be an Elder."

Dread filled Betsy, but she threw up emotional walls, finally understanding Pearl's request as more than idle talk. "So, the bugs gave her sensing ... or she comes by it naturally. Have you figured out what else she has?"

A loud laugh filled the room. "I hope you're kidding. We just got here a few minutes ago. We've barely had time to settle, Betsy. I don't know why you'd think we'd have time to do anything else."

"Right, sorry." She shook her head. "Well, we have some time over the next week while we first go to Torville Station Number Six and then to whichever planet Yav'til took Dulaine."

With a grunt, Pearl pushed herself up. "Why do we need to go to the space station? Can't we just go after Dulaine?"

Betsy started to pace the small room. "I forgot you weren't aware of the plans." She spun on her heel at the edge of the space. "Though Balzeno is certain of where Yav'til took your sister, it would be nice to double check the surveillance. We only have Viera's memory. And though I love her like a sister and trust what she said, I'd like to see everything myself. Planets are far spread. If everyone is correct that the dark elf took Dulaine to Qazah, well, the space station is more or less on the way, only about four or five days off course. It will allow the chanzii to restock on all of the things we will need for the round trip."

A tension filled Pearl's body. "While I appreciate the due diligence, can't Violet do the restocking here? Can't the qynads help out?"

Zuza leaned back on his hands so he could see both of them. "Yes and no. They can restock some of what the ship needs, but in the end they don't run the same kind of ship the chanzii do. The space station is better equipped to help out. Also, the closer to Qazah we restock, the better off we are for that return trip. There won't be any place to restock near that planet."

Pearl grumbled. "I really want to help Dulaine. I have no idea what they're doing with or to her. I hope she's okay."

"Me too," Betsy said, "me too."

After lunch, the three headed to a training room. There was a table and two chairs. The first thing they did was have Zuza read Pearl's magic.

"Okay, I want you to think of opening up your magic, letting it flow for just a moment, then closing it all down. Don't open it up for too long. It doesn't take much for me to read."

Pearl nodded then shut her eyes.

Both Betsy and Zuza waited. Nothing happened. They looked at each other, then at Pearl. Finally, Betsy shook her head. "Do you have any idea what you're doing?"

"No," she said, laughing. "I'm trying to imagine my chest like a cabinet. Then, I want to open and shut a door quickly."

Betsy shrugged one shoulder. "That isn't too bad of an analogy. When you're doing your magic in Oz, do you think of your magic that way?"

"Yeah, I like to imagine magic being contained in drawers, and I can open it up when I want to use it. Each component is neatly arranged in its own place, organized and separate."

Betsy had never heard of, or thought of, magic being kept in anything like that, but a mental landscape was just that, a mental game to help the practitioner to control the power they had inside. "Okay, close your eyes. I want you to imagine yourself in a library, or kitchen, or some room that has a large cabinet with many small drawers."

"Oh!" Pearl said, perking up. "I love the idea of a library with a card catalog. My friend, Cassidy, she uses an old card catalog for her make up case, well, part of one at least. It's really neat." She bobbed back and forth in her seat, as if dancing.

"That's perfect." Betsy tried to speak with a soothing tone. "Now, imagine one of the drawers as being a bit bigger. That will be the one that contains the soul of your proficiencies. Do you see that one?"

A small crease formed between Pearl's eyebrows, then she nodded. "Oh, yeah, there it is. Near the bottom. A longer drawer that is as wide as the cupboard is."

"Okay, perfect. Now, open that drawer, leave it open for a count of three and close it."

A wash of magic filled the room. Betsy backed up to a wall to brace herself. She saw Zuza close his eyes, hands waving back and forth, palms down, then palms up, as if trying to absorb what Pearl had released. It felt like the magic filled the room for hours, though just as soon as it started, it ended. She had to lock her knees to stop from sliding to the floor.

Gods above, when those bugs do something, they do it with oomph.

Pearl's eyes opened and she smiled. "Did it work this time?"

It took an effort, but Betsy forced herself to laugh. "Yes, it worked. I probably should've told you to only release that for one or two seconds."

They both turned to Zuza, who continued to sit with his hands out, bobbing his head slowly up and down. After another few seconds, a small smile spread on his face and he looked at Betsy. "Well, we were right, she has imbuement as one of her proficiencies. That town is a marvel. The dwarves are going to bug-nap the lot of krottel just to have more imbuers in the galaxy. Her other specialty is liquid."

As if watching a tennis match, Pearl gazed back and forth between them. "What does that even mean?"

Zuza shrugged. "At first, not much. You can work with things that are liquid. Eventually, you can work with other states, like ice and gas."

"I can manipulate water?" Pearl sounded excited.

Betsy snorted. "Amongst other liquids, yes. And please, don't make it rain on this ship!"

They spent the next few hours working with Pearl to start to understand what it meant to be a wizard versus a witch. After, she headed off to shower. Her need for a magical soak was even more important after that amount of magical output.

Once she left with Zuza, Betsy looked at the room and chuckled. "We're going to need a clean-up crew every day to clean and dry this floor!"

17

I'm Ready For My Close Up

Betsy

Since leaving Earth, Betsy hadn't seen Violet much. As ship's captain, Violet woke early, got ready for her duties, and headed off to the bridge. There were a few days she let her second run the ship, but those days were few and far between.

When they'd left Earth, both knew they wouldn't see each other much. Their time together would be limited to cuddling in their sleep and whatever meals they could share. This morning, Betsy had arranged to have a couple of hours before they reached the space station.

Rolling over, Betsy wrapped her arms around Violet, intertwining her legs with the other woman.

With a sound that could have been a purr, Violet rolled her hips, then smiled as Betsy dipped down for a sizzling kiss. After several moments in which Betsy lost herself in the feel and heat of the woman below her, she pulled away. "Morning, sunshine."

"Morning, fire cloud. Are you going to burn me with your heat to wake me?"

Betsy groaned, a smile hurting her cheeks. "That was awful, but yes, that's the plan. Now, behave so I can ravish you."

Violet sighed. "If I must."

"Oh, I believe you very much must." Her voice was low and husky. "My tongue has been tingling to trace every inch of your body, and I feel that now is the perfect time." Slowly kissing and swirling her tongue down Violet's neck, Betsy slid her body down, swiveling her hips back and forth.

As Betsy licked her way to Violet's voluptuous breast, her hand skimmed down the other woman's silky-smooth body, landing on her hip, tracing circles along her lower belly.

By the time she reached her first goal, circling with kisses up to the nipple, Violet writhed below her, moaning. Panting, her hands entwined in Betsy's hair.

Betsy sucked in the nipple, flicking her tongue over the tip. She dragged her teeth over the sensitive end, enjoying the feel of Violet's movements below her and her tiny mews.

Once her breathing roughened and her head fell back, Betsy continued her exploration down the sculpted body, reveling in its perfection.

At her thumb, still teasing with its slight motions, Betsy paused. "Hmm," she hummed. "If I'm going to taste all of you, I should move down to your feet and work my way up, shouldn't I?"

Violet bucked up with a groan. "You're going to kill me. Just remember we have years and years." Betsy leaned down for a quick lick, wondering how well she'd be able to hold her thought. Violet gasped, then growled. "Years of retribution, Elder. Years."

Laughing, Betsy dipped down once again. While her tongue circled and flicked Violet's most sensitive area, bringing a series of sounds that went right to Betsy's core, she slid her fingers into Violet's slick heat, probing as the other woman squirmed.

Betsy knew this wouldn't be a quick process, but the sounds and motions did things to her, too.

Under her, Violet quivered then her body tightened. She gasped, "Gods, yes! Yes, yes, yes, please, yes, Betsy, yes, yes!"

In an attempt to prolong her orgasm, Betsy continued to stimulate her turquoise goddess.

I could spend a lifetime learning this body.

Zuza promised to take Pearl to the promenade. He knew she'd be nervous and the emotions of that many new people would be hard for her. Sharing the sensing proficiency, Zuza could help her to navigate the large space full of new sights and aliens.

Betsy thought there were very few things better than a meal in a galactic space station and the chance of Pearl being overwhelmed was worth the experience.

Xantay joined them. Both Juniper and Violet had to oversee the maintenance of the Hoftil and were ship-locked.

That left Betsy to do what she did best, be a nuisance to those in charge. She'd spent a year living on this station. It had been several lifetimes ago, but unlike a city on Earth, things didn't change much. More than that, though some of the aliens had shorter lives, many didn't and she recognized some of the beings she interacted with.

It took some work, but she finally got to the head of security. The group who headed the prestigious position was a team of aliens, including an elf, a dwarf, and a qynad. Two of the three had been in the same position when she'd lived on the station when she'd been so much younger.

A deep voice echoed from an opened door. "Pillar Doeth, enter."

She smiled. "E'fon, is that you?"

The dwarf sat at the far side of a dark mahogany table. His long beard, braided with beads to represent his station and role at Torville, dipped low, below the level of the table. The rest of his hair was tied back in smaller braids. The dim light in the room hid the red from his locks, making his hair look brown, like his eyes, which crinkled in recognition as she entered. "It is me, and when did you get to be so old, child?"

"I'm not a child, old man! And, according to Elder Balzeno, I'm an Elder, I'll have you know!"

E'fon threw his head back and laughed. "Why, so you are. I can't believe how the time has flown by. And you waited this long to stop by?"

Next to him, tall and willowy, sat Saph'elle, a dark elf. She had to be the elder of the two, though Betsy wasn't sure. The twinkle in her clear gray eyes was the only thing that showed her amusement. "Tell us, youngling, why come barging into our domain?"

Betsy had told each and every layer of security exactly what she wanted. She knew these two knew. "Have you already reviewed the tape?"

Both of them smiled. Saph'elle shook her head. "We have not. We thought we'd wait for the infamous Elder from Earth to join us. Come, sit. Order up some coffee for all of us first. Then we shall see what happened on the promenade all those days ago."

After doing as directed, one of the panels began playing the video surveillance from the day Viera and Scout waited for Tiffany and her family to meet up with them. As soon as the two security chiefs realized that indeed Yav'til, the infamous dark elf, wanted throughout the galaxy, sat at a table adjacent to them, they both stiffened and made disapproving noises.

"Add sound, table 7E," Saph'elle demanded. "And I need an explanation of both how he got on our station, and why no one noticed a phoenix sitting at a table speaking with a dark elf."

Betsy sighed. "Viera noticed, but she didn't know it wasn't supposed to happen. I want to know how she understood what they said."

Sound started playing from a speaker. Betsy listened but was unsurprised when she didn't understand a word either said. At the next table over, she watched as Viera's eyes widened and her jaw dropped. Her friend clearly understood every word.

At the end, Saph'elle snarled out words Betsy assumed to be swear words. "Again, I don't know what was said. The translation didn't pick anything up."

E'fon slumped. "The technology was never programmed to pick up the dark elf native tongue, the original language of magic."

Betsy nodded. Balzeno had said as much. "But both of you understood?" They both nodded. "And what my friend Viera, the Earthling sitting there—" she pointed at the screen, "said, was a factual translation? That elf kidnapped a girl from Earth and took her to Qazah to help him reestablish his testing on the tuvan?"

Face tight, E'fon nodded. "Yes. I'd like to speak with this Viera."

Betsy shrugged. "She's on Abritos. You'll have to put a request in with Commander Firoza."

He didn't look happy. "Why did she leave without making sure to communicate with us?"

"She's not used to our, or your, ways. She's new to galactic travel."

"Isn't she an Elder? Elder Kor, right?" Saph'elle tilted her head, as if trying to recall everything she could about Viera.

"Yes, but if you recall, she's the one the krottel kidnapped."

Both their faces tightened. E'fon snarled. "Is that what they do when they open up the wizard in a being? They bring about three, not two proficiencies? And because of the original way Elder was defined, these krottel, by definition, have created 'superior' magic users."

Saph'elle scoffed. "It's the yonat all over again. Beings of magic, moving up the magical ladder way too fast. No offense, Elder Doeth, but even you, at your age, have progressed quickly. How old are you again?" She waved her hand. "Never mind, it doesn't matter. The point is, 'Elder' should be more than the number of magics you have boiling in your gut." She spit the last out with a practical snarl.

Betsy remembered when she was here as a youngling, just turned one hundred years old. Her dad told her that both Saph'elle and E'fon were from families of elves and dwarfs who had specialized in a single proficiency. They were excellent in that one, but it would be a mind-bogglingly large number of years before either of them mastered a second, much less third proficiency. By all rights, they were old and powerful, but their magic wasn't diversified.

Wizards like them often did jobs like security. Few could battle them and win. But they rarely, if ever, got the honorific of Elder.

Betsy nodded. "I completely understand, and agree, with what you've said. It always seemed odd to me that the number of proficiencies you had, but not what you mastered, determined your title. Not to mention years of practice. After Viera, er, Elder Kor, was given her title, she bristled almost as much as you are now. To her, she doesn't even feel right with the title of Pillar. She'd prefer student, probably for several years."

Saph'elle's face softened. "That's good. I mean, she has the title, it's hers. But I'm glad it hasn't gone to her head. I'm glad she didn't think to try to chase Yav'til down."

"No, the only reason she'd have even followed him was to get the girl back, but she called me first. I advised against going after the dark elf. She's too new to her proficiencies. She agreed and returned to Abritos." A storm brewed in the security captains' faces. Betsy held up her hands. "I didn't know that neither she, nor the crew of the chanzii ship had informed you of the intrusion. My guess is they thought the alarms meant you knew."

While Saph'elle sat ramrod straight, E'fon slumped. "That alarm had to do with a couple of phoenixes trying to steal from a fing establishment on the other side of the promenade. We had a security complement circling the area. They may have gotten to the—" He stopped, slapping his head. "Gods below, it was a distraction, wasn't it. I can't believe how moronic I've been. All this talk about Elders. Well, I certainly don't deserve that title."

Betsy felt bad for the dwarf. "It was an honest mistake. You didn't have all the pieces. You do now. As do I. I'm going to return to my ship and we're going to head out."

Both security guards gazed hard at the screen, as if they could memorize which phoenixes to go after.

Saph'elle pointed. "That one. He visits all the time. We can question him."

As the two took notes, distracted by what they watched, Betsy backed out. It was time they got back on the road, so to speak.

She took a detour onto the promenade and found the group from the Hoftil. "Okay, troops, it's time to go."

They gathered their food and paid. As they walked, Pearl leaned in. "Did you know that the people here are obsessed with Vegemite?"

As she asked the question, Pearl grimaced and a tremor of disgust ran through her body.

But It's Red!

Dulaine

As Dulaine gazed at her reflection in the mirror, she wondered once again how long she could stay in the bathroom before someone realized she was missing.

I wonder if my family is still looking for me? Am I a cold case? Unsolvable because I'm not even on Earth? Will they ever give up? Do I want them to? I don't want Mom or Dad to suffer. How could they find me all the way out here?

Dulaine's new morning routine included getting dressed, then rubbing her imbued pebble like a worry stone. She reset the magic every day to ensure her mind was clear of any influence either Max'ina or Yav'til could try to set on her. She knew if she could go through the emotional turmoil of thinking about Oz, her parents, and Pearl, it would hurt, but it meant the stone worked.

She slipped the smooth safety net into her pocket, and splashed her face, making sure there was no evidence of emotions left behind.

Ever since Yav'til had come to the house, he had been her most common breakfast companion. A few times Max'ina had returned, but that wasn't as usual.

Dulaine always braced herself in case it was the man. He was ... nice. He was like that neighbor who didn't have kids but acted like he did. He was nice and funny, but no one wanted to be left alone with him. Not that he was mean or scary, he was just ... odd. It was like he didn't know how to behave around other people.

I wonder if he's alone a lot. Maybe he just doesn't know how to speak with others. As sad as that may be, Dulaine, it isn't your job to socialize your jailer! She shook her head, rethinking arguments that had been circling her mind for days.

With a sigh, she headed out for food.

"Well, you were in there a long time, weren't you?" Yav'til's voice was light and jovial.

Dulaine clamped her jaw down hard, not willing to answer him. She just slowly made her way to the table and sat. She found the quicker she ate, the sooner she could get outside, and the less they spoke.

He chuckled. "I'm sorry, I guess speaking about a woman's preening habits isn't exactly polite. I just never know what you all do in the bathroom. For me, I go in, do my business, wash my face and hands, and I'm done. What else is there to do?"

She sipped her tea and took a bite of the breakfast sandwich. Once done, she gazed across the table at his wide smile. "Are we doing more magic today?"

If possible, his face got happier. "If you want. I know you love spending time with the tuvan, and our lessons have been keeping you from your four-legged friends. But, if you'd like to spend time learning something new, then I'm willing to teach you."

There was a moment of silence, then Dulaine took another bite of her food. *He isn't that great at teaching, but his theories are interesting. If I can take what he teaches and adapt them to what I've learned in the past, maybe I can figure out something powerful.*

"Is there any way I could get something to take notes on?" She'd asked before, but he'd always ignored the question.

"Child, you can't have access to technology. You know that. You're smart. I can tell, even in our short time together."

She clenched her jaw. *Yes, I'm smart. I'm starting to wonder about you, oh jailor.* "Right, but do you have paper and pencil, or something else that isn't electronic? Or are you so advanced that the only type of notes you can think of are ones that are electronic?"

His face tightened. "Let's head outside for your lessons. I have some ideas for what we can work on."

For some reason, she didn't like the expression he made, or the way he stomped to the door. Once they were outside, he began to turn away from the field, then paused, swinging around to the path she took every day to see her colorful, horned friends.

The hour walk was long. Max'ina at least told her about the trees and birds. Yav'til just walked without any of the grace Dulaine expected. With his long legs, she practically had to run to keep up.

On the trek, her mind wandered. *As lovely as the tuvan are, I hate it here. Everything about this planet is horrible. I just want to go home and not be with this stranger who tries to be all clever and isn't.* She wiped her eyes before he saw her emotions. Dulaine had worked too hard to hide the fact her mind was her own.

Once at the field, they sat. "Okay, we've been working on getting you more fluid in your ability to imbue different items."

She nodded. "I've gotten to the point that I can work with almost everything in this field. I can turn them into one-shot wands, so to speak."

"What is this ... wand?" His nose scrunched up.

I should see if he has cards. He doesn't have a poker face at all.

"Well, I can get a stick to turn something like the crackers Max'ina brings me into cookies. But it only works once."

"Yes, yes," he snapped, waving his hand. "I understood the one-shot part. What is a wand?"

"On Earth, where I'm from," she slowed down her explanation. She knew she wasn't supposed to have a perfect memory of everything. In an attempt to play up her memory loss, she scrunched up her face as if trying to pull something from a deep abyss. "Well, a witch, in make-believe, uses a wand—a kind of stick that enhances magic, to help cast a spell."

His eyes narrowed. "In make-believe. It isn't used for real?"

Dulaine tried not to smile as she shook her head quickly back and forth. "No. No one I know uses any kind of prop." She furrowed her brow, as if trying to think really hard. "At least, I don't think—"

"Never mind." He snapped out. "It doesn't matter. We don't need wands, we're much too powerful." His face transformed, a smile slowly spreading. "What I'd like to work on are two things. The first, of course, is the 'one-shot' as you so eloquently put it. But I'd also like to work on something that can be used repeatedly. A one-shot is too limiting."

She shrugged. In the back of her mind, she knew this was coming. Why spend so much energy creating something that only worked once?

He watched her, and when she didn't give a big reaction, he gave a curt nod. "You understand or predicted as much. Good."

A nudge came from behind. Gazing up, she saw Red had come over, looking for food or attention, or probably both. Dulaine reached up to scratch him. He just nudged her more, almost knocking her over. His horn, golden and twisted, came close to her face. She had always avoided touching it, not knowing if the thing was sensitive.

"Hmm," Yav'til hummed. "Do you think you could imbue that?"

"What?" Dulaine didn't see where he pointed.

"That. You know, the beast."

Her heart sank to her gut, and it felt like the world fell out from under her. He couldn't mean what he asked. He wanted her to try to lay a spell on the tuvan? It didn't make sense. What possible reason could he have for wanting her to do that?

Her head hurt trying to think her way through his illogic. "Why? To what end?"

The smile that curled over his face reminded her of the Grinch in the cartoon when he realized he had a plan to ruin Christmas. "Why, child, isn't it obvious?"

"Not to me." The knot in her grew, making her feel sick. Her hands began to tremble and sweat. *I will not harm my friends. He can't make me.*

"It's summer right now. I know it doesn't feel that warm, but trust me, it is. Soon, the snow will start to fall, and food will become scarce. Can you imagine what you'd do for your friends if you could imbue, say their horns, so when they tapped something, it transformed into something they could eat?"

Her first thought was interest, but then she shivered. "What if they bump into a bird or another tuvan? That would be—" Bile filled the back of her throat and she couldn't finish.

"That would be your doing, now wouldn't it? But what if you made the spell a bit more—" he looked up to the clouds, as if searching for the right word, "—sophisticated." He snapped his fingers. "That's it. If you made it with conditions on what would be transformed, the birds and other beasts shouldn't be affected."

Thoughts and ideas swirled in Dulaine's mind. "I would need to test that out on something smaller first. I wouldn't want to place anything on Red that could harm him."

His eyes became ... wild. That was the only word she could think of to describe it. "Don't you think you should test out if you can even place a spell on the horn, first?"

Dulaine squeezed her eyes shut, then rubbed her face. She wasn't sure how the day had gotten to this place, but she really wasn't thrilled about it. "I'm not really comfortable with any of this. I don't want to harm the tuvan."

"I promise you, child, it won't harm the beasts." His face contorted into what she thought of as his 'trust me, I'm nice' look. *I wonder if he practices in a mirror. If he does, he should look at sincere faces to figure out what actual nice people look like.*

Maybe he was trying to convey that he knew what he was talking about. Either way, it put her a bit on guard, though she kind of figured he probably knew more than she did about this topic.

"They're alive," she insisted. "Not things. They can feel and be hurt."

He nodded. "And nothing you do will harm them." The look in his eyes made her wonder if she'd be safe saying 'no.'

He's your jailor, Dulaine—not a friend, not a teacher. He defines the rules of your confinement. Food, clothes, all of it. Her heart hurt for Red, but she didn't want to see what happened when the dark elf got angry.

She stood and wrapped her arms around Red's neck as she whispered, "I really don't want to hurt you, my friend. I hope he's right." Then, stepping back she said, her voice flat, "Fine, what do you want me to do?"

No Rest For The Liquid

Betsy

Betsy, Pearl, and Zuza spent the morning in the training room in the bowels of the Hoftil. They sat on the floor, cross-legged, all facing each other. In the center of them was a glass tub with water.

"You want me to do what?" Pearl asked.

Zuza sighed. "We want to go through a series of low-level spells to determine what you can do."

"Didn't we do this the first day?"

Amusement filled Betsy at the horror she heard in the other woman's voice. "No, dear. We asked you to tap into your proficiency by touching a glass of water, and the thing exploded all over the room. Zuza and I both threw up air walls that stopped both the glass and the water from hitting us, but it did leave the room in quite a mess."

Pearl's face scrunched up and her hands tightened on her knees. "So, you thought it would be a good idea to try this again?" She squeezed her eyes shut and a tremor ran down her body. "Are you sane?"

The laugh that had been building up burst out. Betsy had been trying to hold it back, but the girl's drama was too much. "You have to learn before you do something bigger outside of this room and possibly when we're not there to help."

Her legs flopped to the side, and she gave Betsy a deadpan glare before she spit out, "Fine. What do you want me to do?"

Zuza chuckled softly. "I really wish Ania were here. She would know all of this better than us. But I'm pretty sure we can figure out the first few steps."

As he spoke, Pearl's eyes narrowed. "Do you even know what you're doing?"

The ire in Pearl's voice turned Betsy's amusement to annoyance. She took a slow breath. "Yes. We both know what we're doing. This may surprise you, but we're both a lot older than we look." Betsy waited a beat, but Pearl didn't respond, her look speaking for her. *Right, youthful arrogance. Of course she knew.* One of Betsy's eyebrows rose, despite her attempt to keep a blank face. *Why do so many of these younger generations irritate me so much?* "If you'll follow our directions, we can help you to harness and control this new power opened up within you."

Pearl guffawed, then snapped out, "How long has it been, oh Elder, since you've helped someone as untrained as me learn to wield new magics?"

Betsy's other eyebrow rose to meet the first. "Well, end of March, early April. It's now August. So, about four months." As she spoke, ticking things off on her fingers, Pearl's bluster deflated. "And since Viera and I didn't share any of the same proficiencies, it was a matter of teaching her things I have some skill with," she waved her hand and the water in the tub that sat in the center of the rough circle they made, shot up in a basic column before dropping back down, "but is not one of my specialties."

Zuza leaned back on his hands. "You have to understand, Pearl, right now you have three magics fighting within you to escape. The worst is that sensing. The reason is it was never meant to be so strong ... at least not yet. This is what happened to Viera. You've lucked out that I can help you to harness that. You should be able to play some with your imbuing, since it's a skill you have some background in. We'll help you with the basics, learning how to utilize your own power versus the magic from without, but we really need to work as a group to figure out liquid. It could be amazing, you know."

Slumping, Pearl sighed. "I know, and I really am excited to have gotten this far. I just ... it's a lot. It isn't that I don't want to do this, I'm just ..." Her hands waved around, her mouth opened and shut, and she shrugged.

"You feel like a fish out of water," Zuza finished for her.

Betsy looked between the two of them. He shrugged and tapped his chest. "I can feel it in here. She's beyond overwhelmed."

"Okay," Betsy took in a deep breath. "I can work with that." She finally knew where to begin. As she focused on the place she wanted to begin, Pearl turned her wild eyes to her, emoting strong enough even Betsy could feel her fear.

"Close your eyes." She watched as both Pearl and Zuza followed her directions. Once they did, Betsy closed hers as well. "Find your library with the card catalog. I want you to reorganize that you have three large drawers, one for each of your proficiencies."

"Should the drawers be at the top or bottom, or vertical, separating the cabinet into thirds? How wide can this structure be?" As the questions came, Pearl's voice got higher and faster with stress.

"Shh." Betsy reached over and rubbed Pearl's knee before closing her eyes again. "Make sure whatever you do, it feels right for you and your magic. Don't force the design. This isn't real. It can take on any shape that works for you."

A small giggle had both Zuza and Betsy gaping at the girl. "The drawers, they're ... one is in the shape of a raindrop, one a funnel, and the last a heart. There are smaller drawers around each ... and it looks like there are some that overlap." She bit her lower lip. "Is that wrong?"

Zuza's low voice filled the room, calming in its timbre. "No, dear. There is no wrong in what you're doing." He looked at Betsy and she could hear his mental voice. *Her emotions are calming down. She's gaining control. Keep going, you're doing great.*

She smiled. They didn't often communicate like that, but it was nice to hear him that way.

"Now, Pearl, I want you to make sure that this room, the library, the living room—"

"The apothecary lab," She said, awe in her voice. "It's where magic can happen but is always contained."

"Perfect." Betsy remembered seeing Porter working in the lab, creating the tinctures the family sold. "When you don't have a drawer open, the magic should be sealed away. If, for some unknown reason, a drawer is left a crack open and some of the magic escapes, it cannot get out of the lab. Labs are built to contain what happens inside."

"That's very true," Pearl said with authority.

I wonder if anything has happened in any of the labs she's worked in. "I want you to crack open the liquid drawer, but only a bit. We don't need all of your power, just enough to see how it behaves."

It took a few moments, but when Pearl opened her eyes, a new serenity seemed to have settled over her. "Okay, I think I'm ready now."

Zuza nodded. "That you are. You feel stable."

"Where do we start?" There was a new peace around Pearl, like a blanket, that made everything in the room feel easier, more balanced.

"I want you to move some of the water in that bucket, up the side." Betsy demonstrated what she wanted. As long as they stayed at the basics, she could manage the skills. It was just when they moved up the ladder, so to speak, that she would only be able to describe and not do.

As they watched, waves formed on the top of the water. Then a splash hit the side of the tub. "I can't do this!"

With an effort, Betsy didn't smile or laugh. "How many things have you had to train to learn?"

Her shoulders dropped. "Not many. I tend to pick things up quickly. Why?"

"This is something completely new, and it isn't something you were born with. You'll get to the point where you can learn new skills fast, but we're still in the first days of your magic. Think about Dulaine and the years she spent patiently practicing something she'd never achieve. Channel her calm; it will help. And, unlike her, you *will* get this, my dear."

At the mention of her sister, Pearl's face hardened. "For Dulaine, right. I can do this."

She didn't, not right away. After an hour, nothing happened but choppy water. After two, there were a lot of snarls, but with the determination Betsy knew Pearl possessed in spades, she could get the water to flow up the side of the bucket.

Then they broke for lunch.

Walking the corridor, Pearl asked, "What are the next few skills you want to teach me? It would be nice to contemplate them. Maybe mental rehearsal will help, you know, like in sports."

Betsy approved. "Not a bad idea. I want you to be able to change the form of water, make it colder, ice, warmer, steam, and eventually change its composition."

"What do you mean by that last one?" They were nearing the cafeteria, and Pearl's nervousness grew.

"Isn't it obvious?" Betsy said with a smirk. "I want you to change water to wine."

The Magic Stops Here

Betsy

Violet stepped from the bathroom and headed for the closet. The two of them had so little time together on this trip. Betsy let her eyes travel over the other woman's shapely curves. "Are you sure you need to get to the bridge right away?"

She bent over, searching for uniform pieces. "Yes, I have duties, you know. And why can't I find my belt? I know it's in here somewhere."

Betsy watched as the other woman dug through their mixed pile of detritus that had collected in the small area.

"What is this?" Standing, Violet held up a box.

Though Violet held the object barely a foot in front of Betsy's nose, she took a moment to enjoy the view beyond before answering. Making sure her ogling was obvious, she said, "I forgot, Devlin sent that along." She finally gazed into Violet's sea blue eyes and saw her mirth dancing back. "He said it was a gift. You left before he could give it to you."

Violet reached behind her and grabbed a robe, much to Betsy's chagrin. After tossing the box on the bed, she slipped it on. "Did that just jingle? Did I break it? Did you? Should it have been handled with care? What did Devlin say about it?" The shocked look on her face amused Betsy. She didn't think anything was harmed.

"Why don't you sit your sexy ass down and open the gift up? I doubt he would've sent something delicate without warning me."

She flopped down and crossed her legs, pulling the box to her lap. With a smile like a kid on Christmas, she pulled the top off, then gasped.

"What is it?" From where she sat, propped on her elbow, Betsy couldn't see.

"Gems, a lot of them, and a note. Hold on."

Violet,

I know you'll be busy, but I'm hoping you'll have time and space to do some practicing of your new art. I have attached a few ideas I have for ways you can imbue these gems. I have sent jade if you want to continue with communication.

There are a few dark stones. Hopefully, Betsy or Zuza can help you with identification.

Onyx - a smooth black stone. This one is good for voice amplification. I don't know if this would be helpful where you're going, but the imbuing of onyx is simple. If you want to practice something on your own and are nervous, this is the way to go.

Black Sapphire – black and opaque, with a hexagonal shape. It has a crystalline structure and is about an inch and a half long. I sent more than one, in case you want to do a few trials. This is an amazing stone. Black Sapphire is fantastic at stopping or ending. I've sent two options along.

One is to stop magic. It is complicated, but I believe you can do it. There is a second version that adds a compulsion that the person who the spell is inflicted upon can't drop the gem for roughly an hour. You need to imbed a word to activate or else it will accidentally affect you. Don't ask me how I know this.

Violet snickered after reading that.

The second spell for the black sapphire will stop time around you. It is one that I've been working on with Elder Balzeno. It only works in a small area for a few minutes. I've worked in an activation code of 'time stop five now.' You don't have to say it loudly, but it had to be something you wouldn't say by accident. From our testing, the stone holds on average three iterations of the spell. If it fails, don't be discouraged. You can reset the magic in the gems a few times. It's one of the things I love about working in this medium.

The last thing I've put in the box are some bloodstones. They are dark green quartz with red crystalline impurities. It is the impurities that give it the name. I use this stone for healing. What I've included is a chant that will stop bleeding and do basic curing. It isn't a general healing. It's specifically to work with something more severe.

I hope this gives you something to do during all your downtime.

Your trainer, who is very proud of your accomplishments,

Devlin

Once she got done reading the letter, Violet just gazed at the gift and its contents.

Betsy sat up and gazed in. "Do you need my help to sort out the different types?"

Violet's head shook for a few moments before she spoke. "I think I can figure it out. The onyx and black sapphire do look similar, but Devlin's descriptions help." She reached in and pulled out a piece of black sapphire. "Would it be horrible of me to take the morning off to try a spell, maybe two?"

"I don't think so. We have a few days before we get anywhere and I think that this could be important, too." She reached out and rubbed Violet's leg. "Do you want me to come to observe the magic or do you want to try it out alone?"

"If you're okay with it, I'd like to have breakfast with you and then have you on the bridge. It isn't that I don't want you with me or that I don't trust the crew, I just want someone there in case ... I don't know. I just have trust issues this deep into unknown space."

"I can help out on the bridge. I'm not chanzii. Xantay has more authority than I do."

"But you're an Elder and the others respect you." She gave a small smile.

"Sounds great."

The command center of the ship was a bustle of activity. Xantay shimmied when Betsy asked permission to board.

The acting captain nodded. "Elder Doeth on the bridge. Welcome."

"Thank you, Major Cassia." She crossed behind her chair to the other side.

"Elder Doeth, you're joining us today?" Xantay's cheer made her smile.

"I am. I haven't spent much time up here. Not since Pearl got her magic. I'd like to see how this part of the galaxy looks."

The qynad made a sound like rocks rubbing together. A laugh.

Across the deck, Betsy sat in a small alcove with a table specifically for visitors. The screen ahead showed a series of stars and, to the left, a dark greenish blue cloud. *I should study more about the galactic formations. I bet both Violet and Xantay would be happy to teach me, or even Balzeno. Would anyone mind if I took a picture?*

She shook her head at her own foolishness.

The ship soon passed the odd cloud and all the screen showed was the dark, inky blackness of space.

On the bridge, the officers spoke, giving updates of time, location, direction, duration, and ships status. Most of their conversation was either beyond Betsy's understanding or nothing she needed to focus on. She just enjoyed the hustle and bustle of their work.

As she took in all their action, a word permeated her mind. "...from Saph'elle. It sounds serious. Should we disturb the Captain?"

Betsy shook herself. "Can you repeat that, please? I was focused on ... well, can you repeat it?"

Major Cassia snapped her head to Betsy and blushed. "I'm sorry Elder, I forgot you were here. We received a message from Torville Station Number Six with high priority. It came from Saph'elle. I was debating interrupting Captain North."

"No, let her focus. I'll deal with the security director from Torville. What does Saph'elle say?" The Major hesitated and Betsy got annoyed. "Look, I'm the one the message is probably for. I'm the one who spoke with her when we were at the space station."

They stared at each other for a few moments before the Major finally gave in. "Fine, I'm sending the message to your personal inbox. I don't know if it has high security. I ask that you share with us if it's anything we, as a ship, need to know, for safety reasons."

Betsy nodded. She headed to one of the private conference rooms in the back of the bridge. "If you want to listen with me, Major, I'd be more than willing. I don't think it's personal. That way you'll be getting the message right away with me."

Major Cassia relaxed as she followed her into the room.

They sat on opposite sides of a conference table that could easily support sixteen. Panels lined the walls of the oval room and were worked into a strip down the center of the table. Skimming her hand along the bottom of the table, Betsy felt the ports for charging several different types of electronic devices. She was impressed that they'd secured such high-end furniture for this room.

Once Major Cassia sat, she reached out and tapped the panel closest to her. She found her personal inbox and opened up the audio file from Saph'elle. It only took a moment for the dark elf's melodious voice to fill the room.

"Elder Doeth and Captain North,

"I hope this message finds you both safely on your way to Qazah. When you were last at our humble station and we had a chance to speak to Elder Doeth, she let us learn not only about the scoundrel and wanted dark elf Yav'til, but a ring of phoenixes who were working for different underground agencies, including his."

"After capturing and interrogating one of their members, we have learned a few things."

Betsy shivered at the thought of their interrogation. Once again, the security leads didn't have a variety of magic, but the little they had was precise and mastered beyond just about anyone else. They didn't end up in security on a whim.

"The first item is Yav'til has spent most of his long life since the creation of the yonat on Qazah. It is why he's been so slippery to find. The planet is mostly uninhabited, except for the tuvan, the beasts he bastardized to become the honored Elders."

Betsy held back her reaction to the description of the yonat.

"Over the years, he created an underground kingdom. He has his home, labs, and receiving areas. From what we gather, it's grand and spacious. His best proficiency has always been solid, so moving the terrain to suit his needs wouldn't be a problem.

"Elder Doeth, we need you to not only go in and find your Earthling child, we need you to bring this wanted dark elf in. As an Elder, you have more responsibilities to the galactic council then you did as a mere Pillar of Earth."

This was news to Betsy, and she raised a brow at the recording in defiance. From across the table, Major Cassia snickered at her, obviously seeing her look of doubt.

"We would like Yav'til brought to us, here on Torville Station Number Six, dead or alive—preferably alive to stand trial for crimes he has committed. But either way, we'd like to see his case finally closed.

Saph'elle, security chief."

When the recording stopped, both Betsy and Major Cassia just sat, gazing at the place the recording played from. Neither moved nor said a thing.

Finally, Betsy sighed. "I'll make sure Captain North gets this information." She looked at her watch. "We're scheduled to have lunch together in under an hour."

"Do you think it's possible?" The Major asked.

Betsy scoffed. "Do you think that I, that *we* can bring in a wanted dark elf that has eluded top officials, wizards, and Elders for over a thousand years?" She huffed out a laugh. "Yeah, no. I think they just need a new person or group to blame that this ass is still on the lam and we're an easy target."

Major Cassia's face tightened. "That's what I feared. Well, I hope they put their lack of faith on the wrong ship. I, for one, think they have. You, Zuza, Captain North, Xantay." She ticked the names off on her fingers. "I think we have a stronger group than any of you know, sir."

Pride filled Betsy, though she knew pride wasn't what would win this battle. At the end of the day, what she really wanted was Dulaine. Saph'elle could bite it and her wanting Yav'til could go to Hades. He'd been missing this long—they could find him on their own.

21

A Sweet Success

Dulaine

It was rare that Dulaine came out to the field on her own. After her morning routine, including a few minutes of mental preparation in the bathroom in which she reset the magic into the pebble, she came out for breakfast, and no one was there.

A note was left by her pancakes and sausage saying she should care for the tuvan alone and that Yav'til would join her later. If she wasn't where he expected her, she wouldn't be given this type of freedom again.

She gazed at the words written to her. *Why doesn't he know what paper and pencil is, yet he can leave this note for me? What does he think this is?*

She pocketed the missive, ready to question him or Max'ina later.

Her room, her prison, was on the second floor of the house. The kitchen was at the back of the first floor. She'd only been there once before. It was the second time she'd been left to go to the field on her own. The first time, she'd gone without any treats for the tuvan. Max'ina told her if she did it again, to get some from the kitchen. Agreeing with her, Dulaine decided she wouldn't go without.

In the kitchen, she grabbed the treats and some vegetables on the counter for herself. They were blue with yellow veining and tasted a bit like a carrot. There were five and she took three.

As she often did when left alone, she walked a bit more slowly, really taking in the trees and other plants. This world was similar to Earth in a lot of ways, yet different. The plants seemed wilder and freer ... and a lot bigger. *Maybe it's because there aren't many animals, especially humans, to destroy their savage beauty.*

When she got to the field, she sat at the edge to contemplate magic. Over the last few days, she'd told Yav'til she'd tried to imbue the tuvan horn, but in reality, she hadn't really pushed out her magic. She'd tried in the witch manner, not the wizard way, using the planet's magic, not her own. She didn't think the dark elf knew the difference, and she didn't want to harm her friend.

She knew he'd catch on and demand she work harder. Her hope was to figure this out on her own, without anyone else there to interrupt her.

Sunflower approached, her yellow pelt shiny in the morning sun. The orange of her mane and tail almost glowed as bright as her horn. It looked to Dulaine like the tuvan could float to the sky and become a celestial body herself.

The beast bent down, nosing her, asking for a treat. As always, Dulaine gave her one of the ones in her pocket. Sunflower wasn't as greedy as Red, and once she had her fill, she began grazing on the grass around them.

With a sigh, Dulaine thought about what she wanted. *I want to keep the trust these animals have in me. I want to go home. I want for all of this to be a bad dream ... well, except for the amazing tuvan.*

Imagining a spell, with all the complexity she could add in, she formed the full creation in her head.

A knot of anxiety built in her belly, matching what she imagined her magic would look like if she could hold it in her hands.

All these minor rules and added conditions—if the fae were real, they'd be proud of me.

With a final sigh, and a tensing of all her muscles, she approached Sunflower and tapped her horn. The drain on her power reserves dropped Dulaine to her knees. She grunted, her whole body shaking from exertion.

It took a few moments of not moving, still as a statue on her hands and knees, before she finally rolled to her butt. "Okay, that used up all that I have for a while. I guess it's time to eat and test, not in that order. Though, the veggies I brought won't really fix what I drained."

She took one of the weird blue crunchy things and took a bite. Dulaine pushed to her feet, thinking if she had hummus, it would taste better and help her recover a lot faster.

"Here goes nothing, my sunny yellow friend."

Throughout everything, Sunflower hadn't reacted. Not even a shiver at the magic touching her horn. It made Dulaine wonder if it had worked.

Her hand trembling, she reached the carrot-like food out and lightly tapped it on the horn, in a weird crossing-of-the-swords-like action. The tuvan eyed her suspiciously but continued to graze. Warily, Dulaine bit into the veggie a second time. It tasted like a crunchy candy bar. The sweet flavor of chocolate and nougat exploded in her mouth and she groaned. It had only been, what, about a month? She wasn't sure. The days and nights were different, but, goodness, she missed candy.

Even though a couple of times a week, Max'ina made pancakes, it wasn't the same thing. The syrup wasn't quite right. Nothing tasted how it should. Suddenly, this weird blue thing with yellow stripes reminded her more strongly of home than anything else had.

Tears pricked her eyes, and she quickly took another bite.

In short order, Dulaine ate all three of the carrot-like veggies she'd brought. In her mind, she should have sugar-belly and be feeling sick. But in reality, she'd just eaten a lot of something good for her.

When she dug deep into her soul, she still felt magically weak.

She sat on the ground, legs out and crossed at the ankles. Tired, she leaned back on her hands. A cool breeze ruffled her hair and the colorful array of tuvan played all around her. She tried to relax and let all her worries go. For a few minutes, she was alone and at peace.

This won't last.

Red approached, nosing her for a treat. Laughing, she dug one out and gave it to him while Sunflower grazed nearby.

She heard footsteps and her head snapped in the direction of the house. Even when it was empty, the elves always came from there.

As she waited, she felt her body tense. *I guess 'me' time is over. I knew it couldn't be all day.*

"I see you're with your favorite two beasts." Nearly jumping out of her skin, Dulaine whipped around to see Yav'til approach from the other direction.

Where did he come from? There isn't anything over there.

He sauntered up until he stood over her, looking down. "Have you done anything interesting today?"

It felt like he gazed into her soul, read her mind, knew more about her than was possible. She wanted to search the area for hidden cameras, but there was no way he could've placed any in such a wild wilderness. "I've just been sitting here, relaxing. It's such a nice day, don't you think?"

"It is. Are you hungry? Should we break bread before you try to enspell your red friend?"

She knew what he said was a must. In reality, she worried about trembling if she even stood. That one spell really took it out of her.

His eyes narrowed. "Come, child, let's go find Max'ina. I'm sure she'll have some lunch. Then we can spend the afternoon working on your magic. I have a feeling today will be a good day."

Dulaine wondered if he already knew. Deep in her gut, her worries grew.

22

Trading Secrets

Betsy

etsy watched as Pearl played with her food. She didn't disagree with the subtle disappointed look on the girl's face. Nothing was wrong with what they ate, it was just ... different.

As if feeling Betsy's gaze, Pearl snapped her eyes from the mess of eggs and potato-like substance on her plate to Betsy. "It's ..." She shrugged.

"It's good, but it's subtly wrong, and you miss home and the food you're used to."

Pearl sipped her coffee and sighed. "Yes. I mean, this tastes the same, but everything else ..."

"Well, that *is* the same. Earth exports coffee. It is our biggest money-maker. That and Vegemite."

Betsy watched as Pearl worked through shock and amusement. In her opinion the correct two emotions at learning most of the known galaxy loved the Australian delight.

Violet returned with a refill on both her food and coffee. "Okay, I have a few hours before the bridge expects me. Pearl, I was hoping you could work with me on some of my magic. I know you didn't do much with gems, but you do understand the basics of the skills. I've been flooding one of the rooms with magic, so I can practice the imbuing spells Devlin sent. I can only do this one more time before our reserves are too low. I want to make sure I'm getting the most out of what I'm doing if I'm using up the ship's magical backup."

Pearl's mouth dropped open. "Will we be okay if you do that?"

"Yes, we'll be fine. We'll be at Qazah in the next few days. We'll make sure to overstock there, and no one will suffer. Don't worry."

Betsy leaned back, finishing her coffee, and gazing across the table at Zuza. "We may want to order up some wine—"

"Or something stronger," he murmured.

"—or something stronger," she agreed, "if we're going to be training two people in two magic systems while one of them overrides us with her superior knowledge in one of them."

Pearl smirked, shimmying her shoulders. "As long as you admit I'm superior, I think we'll all get along just fine."

Across from her, Zuza's face dropped into his hand and he groaned. "You did this, you know. It's your fault."

Violet laughed and they all headed down to the training room she'd prepped.

Most of what Violet needed to work on involved her doing quiet, meditative focusing. The witch magic was slow and silent. When they got to the door, Pearl put her hand up and shook her head. "Why don't Captain North and I go in and discuss what she's been doing. Then the three of us can go into the other area. That will preserve the magic she's filled in here and allow her to focus."

Betsy raised her brows in shock and smiled. "Sounds good to me. We can go and set up for your tort—I mean, lesson."

Zuza chuckled.

Pearl glared, before leading a snickering Violet into the first secured room.

When Zuza shut the door to the second, Betsy headed to the panel to begin ordering up the items they'd use for Pearl. Behind her, Zuza paced the area. "These rooms are remarkable, you know that? We can do almost any magic, and it doesn't affect the ship, the people anywhere nearby, or other magic users on board."

"Yeah, when Viera was going through her training with Flower Prancer, I was impressed with how much they did without me feeling a thing. I ended up speaking with Flower Prancer and Thorn later. I guess they utilized an imbued material from the dwarves. Usually it just lines cells that hold wizards who have been arrested, but it can also be used for training magic. It's probably why Saph'elle wanted us to go after Yav'til."

Pearl entered and gazed at them wide eyed. "Why is it that every time I enter any place, everyone stops talking? What are you all trying to hide from me?"

Zuza laughed. "Nothing. We were just discussing the imbued walls in here that keep all our magical workings in."

"Oh, yeah! Captain North was explaining that to me. That's why the magic she flooded into that training space didn't dissipate into the rest of the ship. It's also how the containment units hold the magic that the showers use." As Pearl spoke, her eyes almost glowed with excitement. "Can you imagine the applications? If we could create a portable way to move magic, then the limitation set on beings living on planets would be lifted. It's like oxygen in space suits."

Her joy permeated the area.

"Okay, space girl, time for *your* lessons. Not on imbuing, which you're already pretty darn good at, but liquid."

"Fine, but can we start with turning water to wine? I really could use some wine right about now."

They all moved to the center of the room where Betsy had set up the training materials. "How about we start with converting water to ice? If you can change its natural properties, then we can discuss morphing it into something different and more exciting."

The eyeroll was legendary. Her attempts at creating ice ... not so much. By the end of the lesson, she had created ice and steam, a faster accomplishment than moving the water around the bucket, but she looked tired. "Well, it made sense. It felt like working in the lab at Katz Apothecary. Basic chemistry, you know. Like, really basic." Pearl shook her head. "I think this part of the magic seems much easier."

Zuza started to clean everything up. "That's good, but in the end, you need to learn and master all the bits and pieces." He moved everything to a table and started tapping away at a panel. "You know, you could easily practice some of this in your suite. If you do, make sure to add another soak. Dropping too low on your magical reserves will make you feel irritable and lethargic. The first will annoy us, the second, you." He winked at her sneer.

Once the room was clean, they headed back to the cafeteria for lunch. Pearl looked ready to pounce on anything placed in front of her. They served a dish that looked like pasta with meatballs but tasted completely different. It was one of Betsy's favorites. Pearl was on her second plate before she paused and gazed at Zuza. "This tastes like something I'd get in New Orleans, not an Italian restaurant. It's ... odd. But I really like it."

"The spices are great. If you close your eyes and try not to compare what you eat to Earth foods, you'll enjoy eating off-planet much better. It's why I'm a happier person than Betsy."

Betsy gaped at her friend, then laughed. He wasn't wrong that he seemed to enjoy his meals more than her. He may have been on to something in his approach.

As they ate, Juniper joined them. "Is our fearless leader almost done? She is scheduled to be on the bridge soon."

"Yes, I won't miss my shift, Ensign." Violet sat with a plate of food and a mug of coffee.

"Captain!" Juniper smiled wide. "I didn't see you approach."

"It's crowded in here at this time of day. I'm not surprised." Violet leaned over to give Betsy a quick kiss. Her easy affection, even in front of her people, sent tendrils of excitement and desire to Betsy's toes.

Pearl leaned in, probably to be heard. The noise level had risen in the last few minutes. "How did it go?"

"I think everything worked how we mapped it out. I don't really know and don't know who I could test it on, but we'll think about that after we get your sister."

"Are we close?" Pearl's eyes widened and she leaned in even closer, as if the news would get to her faster that way.

"Not today, but soon. I think probably late tomorrow or the day after we should reach Qazah."

23

A Muddy Situation

Betsy

Two days later, Betsy sat with Pearl and Zuza at the small table in the alcove of the bridge. Violet had invited the three of them to watch as the Hoftil approached the planet where they believed Dulaine was being held captive.

Pearl squinted, as if she could gaze at the spherical green blob on the display and see her sister waving at them, waiting for her pick up.

"Captain, we've done a full scan of the planet. There are life forms, but not many. There is one structure, but the sensors are ... odd. I'm not sure how to interpret what I'm reading."

Before Violet could respond, Xantay grunted. "Send them to my display. Let me see if I can get more."

Violet waved a hand in agreement.

Pearl slumped. "How long has it been?"

Betsy considered her. "Since Dulaine was taken or since we've been on the Hoftil?"

"Um, I guess the second. Since we got on the ship, time has lost all meaning. First there was the language box, and then, well, the days and nights aren't the same on the ship, are they?"

"No," Zuza laughed. "I was wondering how long it would take you to realize that the Abritos day isn't twenty-four hours, it's twenty-eight."

"Goodness, no wonder everything seemed so ... stretched." Pearl shook her head. "So, how long has it been? What day is it on Earth? I can't even begin to figure it out, can you? Have you? Do we just wait until we return and it's a happy surprise?"

Betsy shook her head as she reached into her pocket. "I could calculate it, but I find trying to keep track of multiple timelines can be a pain. Back on Earth, it's hard enough to keep track of everyone's time zone. So, for me, I'd rather just check when I get there. But if you must know." She pulled out her cell phone and went to turn it on.

Pearl's eyes nearly popped from her head and her jaw unhinged. As the display lit up, she began to make small guttural sounds.

Zuza chuckled. "I think you broke her, Elder Doeth. Can all the king's horses and all the king's men put poor Pearl back together again?"

The girl's shock turned to indignation, and she lightly punched Zuza in the shoulder. "I am not an egg!" Then she turned to Betsy. "How in the world ... no, the *galaxy* did you turn that thing on?"

"I pushed the button. You know, the usual way."

Pearl's face scrunched up and one of her brows lifted. "Betsy! You know what I mean."

It took all of Betsy's years of training to not fall from the seat laughing. The next time she was in a meeting with Juk, ready to kill the boy, she'd think of this and it would lighten her mood. "It's one of the dwarven adaptations to the ship. I don't know that we could call and speak with anyone back home, but we can get emails ... eventually. We are pretty far away. And voicemail. As it goes, I haven't been checking." She shifted her focus to Zuza.

"Nope. Mine has been off this entire time."

"Okay, so, how long?" Pearl sounded ready to explode.

"We left Torville Station Number Six a week ago and Earth about a week and a half ago. We're doing well for time, actually. We may be gone for less than a month."

A calculation started behind Pearl's eyes. "Okay, so we left on August thirteenth and Dulaine was taken on July seventeenth. It's now, what, the twenty-ninth? Thirtieth? So, about six weeks. Good God, I want her back. I'm glad we traveled as fast as we did, but I just want to be down there hugging my sister. You understand, right?"

Zuza smiled. "I'm impressed. You really do know your timeline."

"It's my sister. Of course I do."

Violet stood and walked to the center of the bridge. "Okay, crew, we don't know what we'll find down there. We need to travel under the guise of stealth and strength. I'd love to deny Pearl the opportunity to go, but I don't think at this point anything will keep her from her sister. That said, I'm sending two extra security planet side to help keep her safe. I want a dozen of the best guards who can navigate a forest quietly."

She gazed around at her crew and smiled. "Yes, I know that could be any one of you, but we need the best of the best this time. I'm sending both Elder Doeth and Pillar Brzezinski to handle any of the magical attacks. I'll be—"

Major Cassia stood. "You'll be staying here, Captain. I hope that that's what you were about to say."

Violet smiled. "It is. As captain, I realize I need to stay with the ship. Major, it is your job to lead security and make sure Pearl stays safe."

Xantay rose to her feet. Violet shook her head. "Xantay, for now I'd like you to stay on the ship. I know you're invaluable in battle, but until we know there is a battle, your size and coloring isn't the most ... subtle."

There was a round of chuckles around the bridge.

Once everyone knew what they were supposed to do, where they were supposed to go, Violet gave the word, and movement began.

On the lift down, Zuza leaned over. "Why do you have your cell phone on you, anyway?"

Both of Betsy's brows rose. "We're heading to Qazah. I need photos of the planet to bring back for our files."

Zuza shook his head. "I don't know if that's genius or idiotic, but since we have a few minutes as everyone gets ready and suits up, I think I'll go grab mine. The more information we have ... right?"

The group landed about a twenty-minute hike from the structure they had seen on the scans. They didn't dare land closer. Xantay feared whatever confused the scans would also mess up the transporter. There was also the issue of stealth and not being noticed.

The forest was thick with tall trees and wild brush. It felt alive and excited for them to be there. Betsy couldn't quite understand it, but she knew that something about the land welcomed them.

Before they set out, she placed a hand on Zuza's arm. She sent a quick mental question. *Do you feel it?*

His bright blue eyes met hers. *I do. It almost feels like the trees have a message they want to tell me. I just don't understand them. If I close my eyes and wait, just a bit longer, maybe they'll confide in me their secrets.* He shook his head. *It makes no sense.*

At least I'm not the only one, she said back to him. And a look of acceptance passed over his face.

There was a game trail. By the looks of it, the game here wasn't small. Behind her, Major Cassia whispered loud enough to be heard, "We're going to follow the trail. Be wary everyone. Though it feels like we are being welcomed, every embrace can turn into a rejection." She glanced at each member of the party to make sure they understood. "This trail looks wide enough for jestcano. If their creatures are that big, they can easily take us on.

Don't let your guard down because of reports of no humanoids."

Pearl looked confused but didn't ask. Betsy leaned over. "A jestcano is a large six-legged beast on their planet. It sort of looks like a walrus with iridescent skin."

"Got it. Big and scary. I'm assuming her next command is don't get killed."

"Exactly," Major Cassia said. "If you do, I'll have to do all sorts of paperwork, not only on Abritos, but also with Earth, and probably the Intergalactic Council. And I hate paperwork."

After she got done complaining, Pearl laughed. "Fine, if only to save you from a bureaucratic nightmare."

"Thank you," the Major said, sounding very sincere.

Everyone in the group seemed to relax at the silly banter. After that, they started down the trail. Three of the chanzii took the lead, followed by Betsy and Zuza. Then more of the chanzii, Pearl, and the rest. There was a pressure in the air about ten minutes into their walk.

A shiver ran down Betsy's back and she mentally reached out. *Do you feel it?*

With a quiver in his voice, Zuza responded, *The compulsion to leave is strong. The group won't get very far. I can block it for me, and a few of the others.*

We need to combine our magics to make it more. I know it's been awhile, but we need to protect everyone. This is why there aren't guards or sentries. No one makes it more than a few feet in.

The sound of shuffling came from behind, and Betsy knew some of the guards were about to run.

She and Zuza clasped hands. Betsy took the lead, since life was one of her proficiencies. Forming the spell, she pushed out a small wave of life energy built from both her and Zuza's well of power. They created a shell that coated each member of the group, cleaning and protecting everyone from any influences that were left in the air. The spell took a few moments, and when it was done, Betsy shivered at the expenditure of force.

The steps of Pearl and the chanzii got strong again, and she breathed a sigh of relief.

Zuza tapped her shoulder. When she turned, he handed her an energy bar. She had some in her bag, but he got one out first. Relieved at his fast action, she took the needed calories and ate them quickly. She heard talk from some of the chanzii, curious at their needing to eat so soon, but it didn't matter, at least they were still there to critique them.

It took another quarter hour before they got to an open field, alive with a rainbow of ... yonat? No, these weren't yonat, they were the beasts the yonat were created from, the tuvan.

Gazing at the field, Betsy thought this was every young kid's dream ... unicorns of every color scattered around a perfectly green field of grass, bordered by large trees on a bright sunny day. She couldn't believe how pretty it was.

"Dulaine!" From behind her, she heard Pearl before the young woman ran past, darting out into the field, running towards her sister.

Distracted by the animals, Betsy had missed the point of their trip. The rest of them jogged to catch up.

Dulaine wasn't alone. A tall pale elf stood with her, a scowl on his face. Betsy dashed, using the planet to speed her up. She got ahead of everyone, including Pearl. Holding out her arms, the universal sign to stop, she yelled, "Yav'til, return the girl."

"Why, what do we have here? How did you get this far, younglings?"

He threw out his hand. A wave of air, like a wall of tiny twisters, approached. Zuza stepped up next to Betsy and together they dissipated his attack.

With a snarl, he flipped his hand, and plants started to grow all around them, twisting up their legs. The screams from behind told her the attack wasn't just against the two of them.

Betsy snorted. "Are you a babe?" She flicked her wrist as if waving off an annoying insect and continued to walk towards the elf. Zuza stayed by her side.

"You are too young to be able to undo my magic," he spat out.

"Or maybe you're too old, a doddering old fool. You played too hard when you were young, and now you think no one can keep up with you." Betsy shook her head in disappointment. "So many people want to find you, and here you are, weak." She practically spit out the last word.

"You had to get here with a ship, Earthling. You have no idea the ways of the galaxy." His face twisted into a smile, and then the ground shook and he disappeared.

Screams from behind caused Betsy's blood to run cold. Turning, she saw the field bubble and churn as if it were a choppy ocean and not mud and grass. Then, from the ground, elf and dwarf creatures pushed themselves up, made from the rock and soil. The asshole had a field of golems!

"Fall back!" she yelled. "These are magical creations. I don't know what will take them down."

Major Cassia ran up to her. "Can you use your power to unwind this, like you did his other attacks?"

"Not all of them. He filled these creatures over time. It isn't countering a bit of magic; it's months if not years of his power. Call Xantay. Bring any combatants you have. This is going to take fighting. Take off their legs, stop their movement."

"Why not have the ship just bring us up?"

Betsy closed her eyes to think. An instinct. "That's where he's gone. If we're all on the ship, he'll use us as hostages, or he'll eject us out into space. I don't know ... I just know we need to be here, now."

"So we're stranded?"

"No, we have means of communicating. We just need to win this battle first, Major. Can you do that?"

Her face hardened. "Yes, Elder. We can do that."

As the field filled with more troops and Xantay's red form appeared in the sky, Betsy wondered how long this battle would last and if they'd win.

24

What's Mine Is Mine

Violet

The team on the planet disappeared from sensors. Violet felt sick. She didn't want to lose any of them. They were an amazing group, and she had to trust that they'd be okay.

There were still people on board the ship. She still had a job to do.

Every few minutes, Xantay tapped on her console. "Major North, our sensors still can't penetrate anything more than before. Our people are ... well, I believe they're alive, but I can't get more details than that."

"Thank you, Xantay. Keep me informed."

After what felt like too long, her people appeared and Major Cassia's voice snapped out over the communicators, "Send down Xantay and all the troops. This is war!"

Heart pounding, Violet leapt to her feet. She nodded and gave nonverbal commands. Then she tapped her communicator. "What about me, Major?"

"No, we need someone to—"

Her communicator stopped working, replaced by static. A smooth voice spoke from the other side of the bridge. "Don't you know, Captain, you're supposed to go down with the ship?"

Violet turned and saw a tall, willowy, light purple male glaring at her. Her stomach did a flip, but she stood tall. "Yav'til, I assume."

A smile slithered across his face. "All these years and still everyone knows who I am. It's so," he took a deep breath, like smelling a rose, "satisfying."

She hoped everyone got to the planet. The elf had been sought after for centuries. There was no way he'd leave the ship easily. Any of her people left would be fodder for him to do with as he pleased. She would rather him just have her. This ship couldn't be flown with just one person. It needed a crew. If he tried to harm her, he'd be stuck here.

"What's your next move, dark elf?"

"Isn't it obvious? We're going to fly away to a new planet and start over. I have you to help me repopulate. We have this ship. What more could I want."

It was too much. Violet laughed. "That's it, just up and move? The neighborhood has gotten bad, time to relocate?"

He shrugged. "Do you have any better ideas, Captain?"

"I do." She slipped her hand into her pocket and wrapped her fingers around the cool gem.

"And what's that?" His eyes narrowed. "What are you anyway? I didn't see any Earthlings with your coloring when I was collecting the child."

Violet smiled, happy to know he didn't know about Abritos or the chanzii. "Me? I'm the Captain, like you said. And can you catch? *Stuck for time. Web magic hide.*" The last two were the incantations for the gem. She wanted to say them softly, but the gem had to hear them ... or something. This was all new to her and she wasn't sure of anything.

She tossed the gem as she said the words and pulled magic through her. It didn't take much, but she needed some.

As she hoped, his instinct was to raise his hand to block the black sapphire from slamming into his nose. It stuck to his palm, there to stay for at least an hour ... hopefully more. *Gods above, I wish I could've tested any of the magic Pearl and I ironed out. Devlin's notes were amazing, but Pearl ... that young lady has more knowledge than any person her age has a right to have.*

"What did you say? You aren't a wizard; I would be able to feel it. You also aren't from Earth, so you can't be doing their other magic." The dark elf's face got paler, if that was possible, as he realized the stone wouldn't leave his palm. He shook it harder and harder, but the gem wouldn't release. He pulled at it with his other hand ... but nothing.

"I would be careful. Even if you remove a limb, the effects of the magic stay with you. The gem sticking there is only a reminder."

Face contorted, he waved his gem-free hand at her, palm up, fingers splayed, as if tossing a data pad to her. They both waited, but nothing happened.

She slowly approached him as he tried again, waving his arm over and over. Each time he added sound, growling and snarling, angrily trying to get something to work.

Finally, he snapped his gaze to hers. "What have you done to me?" Eyes wide, fear laced through his words.

She shrugged. "I took away your magic. What did you think I'd do? You come here, threaten me. Me? *Me!?* I'm the captain of this ship, Yav'til. Who are you? I'll tell you, nobody. No one knows who you are. We had to ask around, find others, older than dirt, to locate anyone who remembers you. That was the only reason anyone at all knows anything about you. There is a video with your face on it. Do you know how long we had to show it around to figure out who you were? Gods above and below, such arrogance in a nobody." She scoffed. "Your name has disappeared into the journals of obscurity, just like you."

His face contorted and it looked like he was about to attack. She tapped a panel near her. "Transport directive, security override, Captain, seven-three-nine-ace-jorn-pawl."

The panel lit up. The system that only allowed transporter controls to be activated from the one room were now allowing Violet control from wherever she was. "Male elf to B- seven-two-nine." As Yav'til began to disappear, a smirk on his face, Violet added, "High security, no data, or electronic devices. Full sweep."

One of his eyebrows rose, but he didn't look too concerned. When she was alone on the bridge, she slumped. A few of the devices fell to the ground around her. He had more attached to him than she would've thought.

As she contemplated the items, she began a scan of the area. She locked Yav'til's loot in a magic container until Betsy or Zuza could look at them. Thinking of them reminded her of the battle going on down on the planet.

With a tightness in her chest, she looked at the results of the scan. The display said it would take another few minutes to complete.

Jaw clenched, she waited. She needed to get Dulaine and Pearl out of harm's way, then she'd start on the rest. But she couldn't do anything until she knew what was happening on the ground.

One more minute.

25

When It Rains …

Betsy

There were dozens of the golems ... maybe even hundreds. She couldn't see through the forest of them.

All around the clash of weapons on what sounded like rock reverberated through the air. Snarls and yells echoed off their foe as the chanzii guard fought. Betsy dug deep into her well of magic, trying to find the heart of the dwarves and elfin things in front of her, to unwind the spell.

When she saw a creature approach the kids, she'd whip out a hand and disintegrate it. The elf's ability to create from dirt and stone didn't exceed hers, Betsy just wanted to find the spark that allowed so many to fight independently.

"Could you do this?" Zuza yelled from several feet away.

Her focus narrowed as she tried to dig deeper into the center of the beast in front of her. It had the look of E'fon but stood double his width and height. The face didn't have a dwarf's normal animated expressions. This thing just attacked with a stone ax, lined with something that shimmered.

"Make earthen golems that independently know how to fight?" Another part of her mind began puzzling out how to do such a thing.

His laughter moved away as they both focused on the fight.

How many of these things did Yav'til create? How many years did he spend on each one? A spark of magic deep within the elf to her left caught Betsy's attention and she sidestepped to get closer. "What do we have here?"

She pushed her power deeper into the monstrosity. The thing stood a dozen or more feet tall. *At this point, the European metric system would make sense. Four meters at least. Getting into double digits for his height is just rude.*

Another elf approached, and she waved her hand, disintegrating it with a grunt. If the act of destroying them didn't take so much of her power, she'd just take down the lot of them, but Yav'til had poured a lot of magic into a matrix that not only held the creatures together; it allowed them to move, think, and act.

The complexity of the spell, the central workings, were unwinding in the elf who stood as if shocked she'd found his inner brain.

When she had almost reached the center of the heart of the elf, a scream tore through Betsy, reminding her of her responsibilities.

Before she knew what she was doing, Betsy ran towards Pearl and Dulaine. "What happened?" She saw two of the golems near the girls and swore at herself for being so foolish. *How could I lose sight in my main goal here? A few mud opponents? For fuck's sake!*

With a wave of her hand and a scream, she sent out a blast that took down all the mud creatures within a dozen feet of her and the Katz sisters, nearly dropping Betsy to her knees. For a moment, her vision blurred and she stumbled.

Not now. Focus on your duty. You can pass out later. Betsy shook herself, grabbed an energy bar from her inside pocket, and forced herself to refuel.

Dulaine lay on the ground, trembling. Pearl knelt, holding her side. She looked up. "I tried to help. I ... it got through. She's bleeding. Help her, Betsy, please."

"Yes." Betsy nodded, not sure what to do. She could do some healing, but it was never her best skill. "I'll ... yes."

Pearl stood and backed up. "She's my sister. She can't ..." A scared, wild look filled Pearl's eyes. Betsy had never seen the young lady appear so small and uncertain.

Betsy slid the last few feet on her knees to get to Dulaine. She pulled up the shirt and saw a wound, a puncture on her side, deep and bloody. Cloth was handed to her. Looking over, she saw Zuza waving his shirt. "Hurry, before she loses too much."

Pushing the folded material onto Dulaine's side, Betsy saw her hands shook. She took a slow breath to center herself. Deep within her lay the power to heal, she just needed to find it.

The sounds of battle grew. There were more screams and yelling. *Gods, it's getting loud. I need to hurry and get back out there. I should tell Zuza to go ... but I may need him.*

A tear ran down her cheek. *I'm crying? When do I cry? I never cry.*

Another one followed the first, cold and insistent. *Wait, since when are tears cold.*

One hit the back of her hands.

With a shake of her head, Betsy opened her eyes and looked up. Pearl stood, face turned up to what had been a clear sky, arms thrown out to the sides. What Betsy thought had been yells from the field, had really been Pearl, screaming out her anger to the sky.

In response, the skies were opening up.

Pearl had brought the rain.

"Holy hell." Zuza whistled. "That girl has some power."

The rain went from drops to a torrential downpour. Lightning struck.

Before Betsy knew how to react, Dulaine and Pearl transported away. She toppled face first into the mud and laughed. She pushed up and tried to clear the muck from her eyes. Behind her, she heard Zuza laughing.

"Remind me never to upset her." He clasped Betsy's hand and placed another rag in it. She gratefully used it to wipe her face. "Look, her storm is melting our enemy. They'll probably reform once they can, but the mud isn't solid enough for them."

The scene would've been gruesome, except all their enemies were mud and rock, and they just dissolved back into the ground. They were left in a very brown field, speckled with tuvan. The creatures had hidden in the trees, but as the battle settled, two of the beasts came out to investigate.

Betsy watched as they sniffed, then trotted over to where they stood. Smelling the air, they snuffled the ground around the spot Dulaine had been. One was red with splotches. The other mostly yellow and orange. The yellow one came over and nuzzled first Zuza then Betsy.

Zuza scoffed. "They're tame. It's like this one wants us to feed it."

"I bet it does. I'm guessing this is what Dulaine was doing out here. She's probably befriended them, given them treats. You know that was the point of Yav'til bringing her here. Magic on these creatures. I'm sure it starts with gaining their trust."

"Huh." His head bobbed. "That would make sense." His eyes danced. "Do you think her parents would freak out if we brought them home as pets?"

A laugh burst from Betsy. "But, Mom, they followed me home ... can't we keep them?"

"Exactly." His smile was infectious. "And if they are really against it, we can take them to the magic school. There's enough ground for them to run there."

"Sounds good to me. We just have to convince the others." A horribly excellent thought occurred to her. "And can you imagine Flower Prancer's reaction to seeing them?"

Betsy didn't get much warning before she was on the ship. Apparently Violet wasn't as adept at transporting people as Juniper, and the Ensign had been hurt badly enough that she'd be with Dulaine in the medical wing for a few days.

As soon as she was ship-side, Betsy showered and changed, then zipped to the infirmary. She saw Dulaine on a bed talking with Pearl. "Hi, Dulaine. I didn't think you'd be awake and speaking. How are you doing?"

Her smile lit up the room. "The Captain transported me and Pearl to the bridge. It was really weird. First we were in the rain, then bam, bridge of a spaceship. I mean, have you ever just been beamed anywhere? And then to be looking at a ... a blue alien with purple hair?"

Betsy smiled at the girl. "Next time you see my friend Viera, you should talk to her about her experience. I think you two would have a lot in common."

Pearl chuckled. "She'll take forever to get through the story. One of the gems Devlin sent, the bloodstone, can stop bleeding and do some basic healing associated with the blood. After Captain North and I discussed what she should work on and what she'd already done, I told her to keep the stones on her at all times. There is some rationale to this. First of all, why create them if they're locked away? Second, you can do tiny pushes of general magic throughout the day to strengthen the power within the gems. It is how Devlin gets his higher-level imbued objects to work as well as he does.”

“Really? Constant recharge?” The idea intrigued Betsy.

“More or less.” Pearl bobbed her head, thinking. “On the ship it’s a bit tricky. There isn’t the blanket of magic, as you all keep reminding us. However, I thought it would be a good practice for her to be in.”

“Well, I’m glad. It seems the gem really worked.”

Once Betsy was certain Dulaine would make it home to her parents, she headed up to the bridge. “Permission to enter?”

Violet’s smile warmed her to her toes. “Elder Doeth, permission granted. I was hoping you’d come. There is a conference in room two to discuss what we’ll do next.”

“Sounds good.”

In the room, she found Zuza already there. “I wonder if she’s going to invite Pearl. I know she doesn’t want to leave Dulaine, but this may be important to her, as well.”

Zuza shrugged. "I don't know, but it may be worth mentioning."

It took about a quarter hour for Violet, Major Cassia, Xantay, and Pearl to all be gathered around the table.

Violet leaned back and smiled. "I'm not sure how we did the impossible, but we did. The ship will leave orbit in about an hour, once all our magical reserves and practice rooms are at full power. Until then, we need to all be debriefed and make some big decisions."

Pearl raised her hand. Violet lifted an eyebrow but nodded. "Dulaine said there was a second elf on the planet. Someone who cared for her, made her food. She thinks this elf was there under duress."

Violet nodded. "I found her after I did my second scan. When I started bringing all of you up, I grabbed her as well and placed her in a holding cell. We can get her story on the way to Torville Station Number Six. Either we, or they, can decide what happens."

Pearl looked like she wanted to say more, but Betsy stopped her. "It's okay. I'm sure this elf isn't surprised by her capture. If you want, we can speak with her over the next several days of travel. Also, before we all forget, you should expect the Torville Station guard, both Saph'elle and E'fon, will want to speak to Dulaine. Being one of the only people to be held by him and escape, they'll want her full story. I'll make sure that you, and hopefully me or Zuza, are there with her as well."

She nodded. "Okay. I don't like it, but I understand."

Violet tilted her head. "I wonder if we can get some of those interviews started in transit. We have the technology and it isn't like it's an interrogation."

Betsy nodded, loving the idea. Anything to get them home faster was good.

Major Cassia looked around the group. "That fight down there was odd. The elf was old and had been living on Qazah for centuries. From what I understand, he had an underground home that spans much of the planet. Are we planning on searching any of it?"

Violet sighed. "I know we have finders' rights to his stuff, but in my opinion, no. We came here for the girl. I don't know that I care about an old elf's possessions."

"What if he has treasures? We could become rich." The Major's eyes widened in excitement.

"He may, but in all honesty, think about those mud men. Anything he has is probably layered in magic and other traps that can and will kill. Is it worth it?" Betsy gazed around the table and shrugged. "Honestly, I don't know that anything Yav'til found over the years would be all that wondrous or valuable to me."

Finally, after contemplating her words, Major Cassia agreed.

Once that debate was settled, Zuza leaned forward. "So, Captain North picked up the second elf. What about the tuvan Dulaine befriended? Are we going to bring them, too?"

Vegemite, It's a Fing

Betsy

It took a week to travel to Torville Station Number Six. Dulaine spent most of the time in the storage area that had been set up for the two tuvan. She introduced Red and Sunflower, as she'd named them, to Pearl, Zuza, Betsy, and a few of the key members of the Hoftil crew.

When she could be pulled away from her four-hooved friends, she and Pearl spent time together practicing magic. If nothing else, Yav'til did a decent job teaching Dulaine new tricks. Though they didn't share sensing, they did share the other two proficiencies and could work together on them. Because of Dulaine's time with both Balzeno and Yav'til, Pearl finally was getting some introductory lessons in imbuing.

On the second day, Betsy got a hold of Saph'elle.

"Elder Doeth, I'm glad you found a way to contact us. Was your journey successful? Did you capture Yav'til?"

Next to her, Zuza squeezed her knee, letting her know he supported her. She knew he could sense her spike in frustration. "I'm glad you asked about the Earthling girl, Security Chief. We did find her, and she seems to be hale and full of spunk and energy. The time on Qazah doesn't seem to have harmed her much."

Over the video feed, Betsy saw Saph'elle's face tighten. "Right, the child. The one Yav'til took from your planet. I'm glad to hear you found her. Is there anything else you'd like to tell us about her? When will she be able to give us a report on her capture and time with the dark elf?"

This was what she expected, what she'd warned both Dulaine and Pearl about. "On Earth, Dulaine is considered a minor. She wouldn't be expected to speak with you or E'fon without an adult. I ask that when you consult with her, her sister, and either me, Zuza, or Major North be allowed to be with her."

The look Saph'elle gave Betsy could shoot daggers. If they were in the same room, maybe Betsy would worry. "Of course, Elder. I would never expect to speak to a youngling without an adult."

"In that case, I explained the situation to her and she's ready whenever you want to schedule the questioning."

The only acknowledgement the security chief gave was a light nod. "Very good. I'll speak with E'fon and send a time to the ship. I expect the child and her representatives to be prompt." She raised an eyebrow. "Now, can we discuss Yav'til? Did he escape? I'm assuming by your avoidance of the subject that he did."

Betsy maintained her neutral face. Zuza's hand on her leg helped to center her. "No, Chief. He didn't get—"

"So, he's dead? Was it you? That can't be right, he was such a strong practitioner. Did you find him dead? No ... well, tell me, what happened."

As Saph'elle spoke, one of Betsy's eyebrows rose. When she finished, it took a moment for Betsy to unclench her jaw. "If you hadn't jumped in, assuming the answers before waiting for my report, you would already know that he was in a holding cell on the ship right now."

"If you put him in one of the Hoftil's cells, you know he's already escaped, don't you? He's just biding his time. I may push up my interview with the child as I don't expect to see any of you back here at the station."

Working hard to maintain a blank face, Betsy shook her head. "As much as your confidence in us warms my heart, Chief, schedule the interview, and we *will* see you in a few galactic standard days. Despite you thinking you know everything, us younglings do have a few tricks up our sleeves."

Before she could respond, Betsy cut off the transmission.

Zuza grunted. "Will you get in trouble for cutting her off?"

"I don't really care." She stood. "Let's go get lunch. She's going to rally and probably set up the first interview for a few hours from now."

"Probably. I can cover it, so you don't have to deal with her."

"Good. I'll work on figuring out Max'ina's story."

There was a full complement of guards when they arrived at Torville Station Number Six. Violet met them at the port opening and led them to the holding cell. Saph'elle and E'fon led the group, smirking, as if ready to prove the cell would be empty.

Betsy waited by the doors. She could feel the dark elf within.

When the station's guards arrived, they threw a magic damping spell over the area. Betsy felt like she was in a pool of caramel, sticky and unable to move easily.

The two chiefs opened the door and the only show of their shock that Yav'til was still their prisoner was the slight widening of their eyes. E'fon stepped forward. "Yav'til, you're under arrest for ... years of misdeeds. We'll list the deeds once you are in a secure cell on the station."

Yav'til's face lit up. "I'm being moved to a station cell?"

"Yes," the dwarf confirmed. "Why?"

"Oh, nothing. I just am tired of being in this one. It's a bit ... limiting. The station is so much more ... freeing."

Betsy rubbed her eyes, but at the end of the day, he was the station's issue, not hers. If he escaped, they could figure it out. She would consult with Balzeno about keeping Dulaine and other people from Earth safe.

Once the guard left with Yav'til and Max'ina, Betsy and Zuza took Pearl and Dulaine to the promenade for a meal.

Violet stood at the junction of the ship and the station, first monitoring as the station guard left, then seeing her crew who had ship-leave exit.

"Just remember, our plan is to leave in four galactic hours. We want to get back to Earth and then let all of you return to Abritos."

Cheers at her words spread through the crowd.

The number of beings in the promenade was particularly high. Zuza leaned down to her ear to be heard over the din of noise. "Our normal place is completely full. What should we do?"

"Let's go to the fing restaurant. It's fancier, but there should be space available."

They navigated through the throngs of aliens. Pearl and Dulaine walked between Zuza and Betsy. Pearl stood ramrod tight, her nerves oozing from her. Dulaine twisted and turned, gazing and gaping at everything she saw. Small sounds of joy escaped her as she recognized new alien species.

Once they reached the restaurant, one of the fings themselves met them and found them a table. They were each handed a menu.

Before Betsy could offer to help, both Dulaine and Pearl began discussing their options.

Zuza smiled warmly at them, amused at their heated discussion over the options. By the time the waiter arrived, they each knew exactly what they wanted.

Pearl shook her head. "I can't believe you got the Earth special. Who has sushi on a taco? That sounds awful."

Dulaine shimmied in her seat. "Then you don't have to have any. I just want something that reminds me of home. I don't care how weird it is."

Zuza held up a hand as Pearl opened her mouth to respond. "It's fine. We each ordered what we wanted to eat. If she hates it, she can eat on the ship. It isn't like any of us need to worry about starving."

"Fine." She rolled her eyes. "It's just that, how many times will we have the opportunity to try these things?"

Betsy shrugged. "You never know. Our world and your lives are in flux. Who knows what things will be like in the next few years?"

The conversation shifted to the aliens on the promenade. Dulaine grew animated as she spoke. "I knew from meeting Xantay that there were dragons ... or qynad, and that they were big, but, my goodness, there are so many varieties, sizes, and colors. It's amazing. I could spend a year just taking it all in."

Both Betsy and Zuza smiled at her exuberance. Zuza nodded. "That's about how long it takes."

"What?" His words snapped her out of her fantasy.

The server stepped in, delivering their food. As always, a small bowl of Vegemite was placed on the table along with a few other condiments.

Pearl's lip curled. "Thank you for your fast service, but we won't be needing—"

"Wait!" Dulaine's hand shot out. "Don't be so rash, Pearl." She nodded to the server. "Thank you, that will be all."

With a snicker and a gleam in its eye, the server bowed and scuttled away.

"Do you like Vegemite?" Betsy asked, trying not to sound anything but curious.

"I don't know." The young girl shrugged, then tentatively reached out a finger, dabbing it in the dark goo, and bringing it to her mouth.

Everyone at the table raised their hands, trying to stop her. Zuza was the most coherent. "It really is better on something, not eaten just like that."

Dulaine shrugged. "I just wanted an idea of what the flavor was. If no one else likes it ..." She dragged the bowl over to touch her plate. Picking up one of her sushi tacos, she dipped it in the Vegemite and took a huge bite.

They all watched in horrified fascination as she ate, a wide smile on her face.

Back on the ship, they ran into Violet in a corridor. Dulaine told her about her lunch.

"Yum! And you didn't bring any back for me? It's my favorite meal."

Betsy held up a to-go bag. "I asked the chef for a special favor. He said he didn't usually do take away, but since he knows Thorn, it would be for her."

A small squeal escaped the austere captain, before she snatched the bag and ran off to their rooms. Betsy waved to the group and followed.

Back in their chambers, Violet sat at the small desk, making fun happy noises as she ate her sushi tacos with Vegemite.

Betsy sat on the bed, thinking about everything that had to be done. "Do you know where the communication stone I used with Viera went?"

Violet's face scrunched up before she nodded slowly. "I think it got put back in the side pocket of your bag. You said you wanted to bring it, not lose it, but not have it in the way."

"Huh, that sounds a bit like me."

She pushed up and went to search the closet. The small area had only gotten worse over the last several days. After digging through all the piles and pockets, she finally found the stone. Betsy squeezed it tight as she returned to the bed.

With a push of her will, she tried to contact Viera. There was a pause with nothing, so Betsy tried again. She wasn't sure if Viera had the gem, what time it was on Abritos, or if the magic even worked from this range.

As she and Violet discussed their day and Violet finished her meal, Betsy periodically sent out waves of intent, trying to reach her friend.

"Hello? Betsy?" Viera's words shocked her out of a story about Dulaine trying to befriend a flock of phoenixes.

"Viera?"

"Oh, my gods! I can't believe we're talking!"

Joy filled Betsy at hearing her friend's voice. She spent the next hour or so catching her up on the adventures they all had and when Thorn should expect her ship back. While she spoke, she heard Violet contacting Devlin and letting him know they'd be back on Earth in about two days.

The Captain then left Betsy, after a quick kiss to her cheek, to start their final leg of the journey.

27

Home Sweet Home

Viera

Children gathered in groups on the different platforms that floated in the field. Viera stood in the center, more of a director, and guide—someone to encourage and help when they got stuck—than a focus for their education.

Each group had everything they needed to learn a topic they were interested in. They'd spend days doing research, finding experts to interview and give presentations, even taking field trips to investigate, in detail, the subject they adored.

When Viera needed extra help on these field trip days, there were always others who were willing to step in and assist. On the off chance she couldn't find anyone, the other children always agreed to join in on learning about something that was off topic to their chosen field of study.

It's like they all know that anything they experience will help them grow, so why not? This love and honor of education fills my heart with hope. I wish it were this way everywhere.

A flock of birds—*r'grazz, Viera, you need to use the right words!*—flew overhead. She watched as they soared in formation across the clear sky. Crossing in a perpendicular direction, much higher, a group of three qynads glided by—a patrol.

So few of the qynads go into military service over technology. Maybe one of the students will study that. I'd love to observe those interviews.

A small smile played on Viera's face.

There was no danger on Abritos. The only people on-planet were the builders, here to prepare for the chanzii coming home. The southern hemisphere hadn't been inhabited by the krottel at all, so the people there were already returning, but in this area, Thorn wanted everything completed before she allowed for repopulation.

Despite that, the qynads had sent five platoons to work with the chanzii. Most of the qynad worked to help develop the planet's technology and help with protecting Abritos for any future invasion. When the qynads took to the skies, they'd been trained to work in groups to do visual sweeps. That said, some of them came to work strictly with the military.

Over the years the two groups, the chanzii and qynad, had formed a strong friendship. Thorn was working with her people to send agriculturists to Grarrou to work there in exchange. She knew finding volunteers wouldn't be difficult.

A bell automatically rang, signaling the end of the day.

All the kids scrambled to gather their items, then one by one they transported away. Soon, the only younglings left were Scout and Tiffany.

The two ran up to her, clamoring to tell her about everything they had learned.

"Whoa, whoa, one at a time!" She laughed, holding up her hands.

"But, Ms. Kor, we can't do this when the others are here. Can't I just tell you now?" Tiffany asked, her eyes wide, begging her. Viera could feel the desperation.

"Of course, I just need the two of you to speak one at a time."

Scout smiled at his friend. "You go first. Are you coming over again?"

He asked her every day. Viera would have to talk to him about it. The question was meant to be welcoming, but every time Tiffany heard it, tension poured from her to the point that Viera's muscles shook.

The young girl licked her lips, then bit her bottom one. "Um, I'm not sure. Did ... um, Ms. Kor?"

Viera wrapped an arm around Tiffany. "I believe there's a job your parents are doing that will take them a bit of time." More than that, if Viera's guess was correct. She knew her thoughts weren't generous, but she believed Tiffany's parents may try to lose themselves again until Tiffany was older. They loved their daughter, but after all those years isolated on Earth, they didn't know how to raise her or be with others. Viera smiled at the kids. "Thorn and I have been given the very distinct pleasure of your company until they're done." She reached over and tapped Scout's nose. "So, no more daily questions. We'll worry about the details, the two of you worry about school and the number of intergalactic mess-ups I can make on a daily basis."

Both kids laughed.

They gathered the last of the stuff and Viera began the closing routine for the platforms. Once done, they dialed up a location near their home.

I have a home ... on an alien planet. No ... I'm the alien here. She gazed at herself, Tiffany, and Scout.

Though Tiffany had changed her appearance to match the chanzii, she wasn't one. *Three aliens walk down a street ...* Viera smiled to herself.

"What's so funny?" Horax's deep voice pulled her from her thoughts, and her smile became a laugh.

"I'm just thinking about how different my life is. I'm still teaching, but now *I'm* the alien. All of us, aliens walking down the street. Different, but family."

Scout shook his head. "I'm not an alien; this is my world."

She reached over to mess up his hair. "I know, but I'm sticking with what I've said. Put us anywhere, we're all family, but ..."

He grabbed her hand. "I get it."

Once they got home, Viera started planning the next field trip. One of the groups had asked about botany. Since most of the planet wasn't inhabited, field trips either involved going to the southern continent, or traveling to a different planet.

I can't believe I'm the same person who never wanted to leave Madison. And, boy, are these field trips better than a bus ride to Chicago!

Once Viera had most of the logistics figured out, she headed back out to the main room to find the others doing their own thing, including Thorn making dinner.

"Hi, sweets, have a good day?" Thorn smiled at her over her shoulder.

"I did. I'm still amazed at how the school runs. I've taught on Earth for years, but this is so different."

Scout scoffed. "Don't worry, Mom, she's amazing. All the students love her."

"It's true," Tiffany added. "Several of the people in my group mentioned how much more they enjoy things now compared to the last couple of years."

Viera laughed. "Well, I know I'm just being compared to off-world education and not other chanzii schools, but I'll take it!"

A strange buzzing came from a bag in the corner of the room. Viera turned and realized it was her purse. She rarely used it on Abritos—it was such a different way of life here.

Horax grunted as he saw where she gazed. "Yeah, your bag has been making that noise for the last hour or so. Do you have an Earth cell phone? Would it work here?"

"No and no. I mean, yes and no. It's turned off." She dug in her purse and found the jade communication stone. Squeezing it, she heard an echo of Betsy's voice.

It couldn't be, could it? "Hello? Betsy?"

"Viera?" She almost dropped the gem as Betsy's voice filled the room. *Goodness, the magic the people at Oz created was fantastic.*

"Oh, my gods! I can't believe we're talking!" She shook her head. "Where are you? Is this reaching Earth?"

"No." Betsy laughed, sounding happy. "I'm on Torville Station Number Six. I'm thinking this is a central hub, about the limit for the gem communication."

"Wow. We should ... I don't know what we should do. It's amazing. Okay, is this just a test for Devlin?"

"No. I wanted to tell you about our adventures and to let you know we found Dulaine."

Viera whooped, beating her fist into the air and twirling in a small dance. The thrill at their success overwhelmed her. Then reality hit. "Wait, you found her, is she okay? She was missing for so long."

"Yes." Viera thought she could hear the smile on her friend's face. "She was being held on Qazah, a planet with tuvan, an animal that looks like colorful unicorns. As it goes, beyond being kidnapped and not knowing about Earth and her parents, she was being well-treated, and her lessons were being continued."

"Too much, too fast. Start at the beginning and tell me everything."

28

Family Reunion

Betsy

A few hours from Earth, Violet contacted several people who would be interested in their return. She knew the ship shouldn't try to arrive unannounced.

Because of her calls, when they all transported into the Athletic Center in the middle of the chanzii neighborhood, not only were Dulaine and Pearl's family there, several of the other Oz townspeople filled the space.

Betsy was a bit surprised to see Kafi and Ania, though not as surprised to see Marco, who had joined Pearl's family rather than the other Pillars. Balzeno, on the other hand, stood amongst the Pillars.

Juk hovered in the corner looking like he wanted to blend in.

Scattered everywhere were chanzii, their luggage in piles along the walls. Betsy smiled and turned to Violet. "I didn't know a group would be heading back to Abritos on the Hoftil."

Before Violet could answer, two flying fluff-balls dive-bombed them, landing on their shoulders. Wes began nudging Betsy's face, demanding attention. Betsy saw Buttercup doing the same with Violet. They both laughed, realizing they had to give the ven their welcome back love.

Once they'd spent a few moments making sure the two rascals knew they were the center of all their love, Violet said, "It was part of the plan. As long as the ship is here, we may as well utilize the space."

"Makes sense."

"I promise you, these two have gotten a ton of pets and scritches at magic school." Kafi rolled his eyes at their antics. "I only brought them because the students don't focus as well with these two demanding all their attention."

"I told you to bring them to me," Ania protested.

Kafi raised an eyebrow. "Betsy said she wanted them back when she returned. If I sent them to you, they'd accidentally get lost in the vast empty lands of Australia. *You* are not trustworthy, Ania."

As they teased each other, Betsy sighed. "So, any emergencies while we were gone?"

"No." Ania said, "Maybe we should send you and Zuza away more often. Things were nice and quiet. Finally settling down into a pleasant routine."

Kafi nodded. "It almost feels like—"

Zuza snarled, "Don't say it!"

"Whatever. We knew this would happen and everyone would eventually acclimate."

Once they were caught up, they walked over to where Pearl and Dulaine stood with their parents. Dulaine gazed from them to Betsy and back again. "What is it?"

Vicki shook her head. "She said she has something to ask of us but can't seem to get it out."

Pearl's face scrunched up. "It's the tuvan. She wants to keep them but doesn't think Mom and Dad will agree."

"The ... tuvan?" Porter asked, testing the word out.

"Ah." Betzy nodded. "I think showing you would be easier than trying to explain."

Xantay sauntered over. "You know, that field where I first met Dulaine would work. Why don't we have Juniper send all of us there? Then we can talk without all of," her head and tail swished in opposite directions, indicating all the insanity of the room, "this."

Violet nodded. "I agree. I'll get that arranged."

It took about a quarter-hour, but they all stood outside the small single room schoolhouse. Balzeno somehow got himself invited as well.

Ania whistled. "Goodness, they look exactly like the yonat. But they're not, you say?"

"Nope, they're just beasts."

Dulaine gazed up at her parents, heart in her eyes. "Can I keep them?"

Porter sighed. "I don't know if we have space for them, love. Where would they live? What do they eat?"

Pearl made an over exaggerated display of gazing around the field where they stood, lined with trees. "What about right here? We can put up a fence. They seem to like the grass."

Balzeno smiled. "I can help with the rest."

Vicki sighed. "If this doesn't work out, then what?"

"Then they get relocated to one of the magic schools," Kafi said.

Once that was settled, Balzeno's eyes narrowed on Zuza. "Now for you, youngling. I expect you to come visit in the next day or two. We need to test that life proficiency of yours. I didn't realize it had gotten that strong. Earth is going to be known as the next hot-spot for Elders."

29

Everyone Deserves A Vacation

Betsy

A few years later...

Betsy and Violet walked around the old chanzii subdivision. Betsy sighed. "Are there any more of your people who still want to return to Abritos here on Earth? I don't know that we've discussed that in a few months."

Violet gazed at the house that had once belonged to Thorn. A child ran out the front door, got to the sidewalk, and darted down the street away from them. His laughter followed him, making Betsy smile.

A few moments later, a man popped his head out the door, and both Betsy and Violet pointed in the direction the kid had run. He nodded, "Thanks. That's the way I'd hoped he'd gone." His eyes narrowed. "Do I know you? You look familiar, but I don't think you live around here, do you?"

Betsy stepped forward. "I'm Betsy. I don't live far, but no, neither of us live in this neighborhood."

His smile widened. "You want to visit one of the old chanzii neighborhoods? See what their life was like when they were in hiding?" His eyes danced. "It's okay, you're not the first. People come by all the time, curious about how so many aliens could've hidden in plain sight."

Violet leaned forward. "Do you think that, living in one of their old homes, you are more attuned to them?"

He shrugged. "Not really. To be honest, except for the ceiling being glass, most of what you have here is just a home. I don't think I'd be able to tell if one of you *were* chanzii."

She nodded. "Pretty sage of you."

"Yeah, I learned after he left, that one of my good friends at work had been one of them. I was really sad to see him go." The man shrugged. "I know they all wanted to get back to their planet, but I kind of wish some of them stayed."

Betsy's brow furrowed. Normally her poker face was better than this. In the years since the krottel outed magic and aliens, since the chanzii learned their planet was available for them to go home, since the Pillars had begun doing what they always knew they'd have to do one day and never wanted to do, it had been pretty well known that aliens would stay on Earth. Most people knew some of the chanzii had remained. It was odd that this was his impression.

Before Betsy could respond, Violet asked, "Why do you think all the chanzii left?"

"I mean, all of the homes here have humans, right?"

With a sigh, Violet shook her head. "No, not all of them. I can think of at least half a dozen homes with aliens. Some don't even try to hide their non-human exterior."

"Oh, you mean the yonat and the qynad? I don't mean them, I'm talking about the humanoids."

"And so am I." Violet waved her hand. "Never mind. I'm glad you are enjoying the neighborhood, sir. It was fun designing them and knowing that they didn't get destroyed will make Commander Firoza very happy."

Before their conversation continued, the two continued on their walk.

Violet linked her arm with Betsy's. "To answer your question, a few who wanted to stay to finish a job now want to return home. They've gotten to an age where they want to settle down and have kids and feel Abritos is the place to do that. Others from the homeland want to travel, see the galaxy, and come here. Earth is an interesting place, especially now that we know our people are so attuned to witch magic."

"That's why Pearl is heading to Abritos, right? She and Marco will become liaisons and educators so that not as many need to come here."

Joy emanated from Violet. "Isn't it amazing? I mean, it started with me and my abilities, but so many other chanzii picked up the magic just as quickly. I love that Pearl and Marco want to travel and visit my planet."

"Well, we should head to the magic school. I think they're at the one in Scotland."

"They are."

Betsy thought about Marco, and how he'd opened up the third magic school in that country because the tuvan seemed to do better in that climate. Once it was determined that's where they'd be living, Dulaine insisted on relocating and training there. It didn't take long for her whole family to follow, including Marco and Balzeno. The dwarf split his time training with the Katz family and pushing the magical boundaries with Devlin.

Finding a transport station, they dialed up the Scottish school. The cool air wrapped around Betsy, and she wished she'd brought a jacket.

In moments, a whirlwind of a teen wrapped her in a hug. "Betsy! You're here!"

"Hi, Dulaine." She laughed. "I can't believe how big you've gotten."

"I can't believe Pearl is going to live on another planet for several years, can you?"

"Actually, I can. I warned you things would be different around here."

She sighed. "I can't wait until I can trot about the galaxy, too."

A chime let Betsy know Viera was trying to contact her. She pulled out the jade stone. "Hi, Viera. Are you close?"

"Yes, we just reached orbit. Are you at your house?"

"No, believe it or not. There's a new school in Scotland. You can find us by the coordinates that Marco will send up to the ship." She signaled the other Pillar who nodded and started typing on the panel.

Once he was done, there was a shimmer, and Viera appeared with Thorn, Scout, Tiffany ... and a baby. Betsy gaped. "You have a kid?"

Viera laughed. "We do. Isn't she beautiful?"

Taking the small bundle, Betsy tapped her nose and gave her a squeeze. "She looks perfect."

Thorn stood over the two of them. "She is. Angela Nicole was born a few months ago. We believe she's just the smartest baby ever."

Violet rubbed baby Angela's purple curls. "How long are you staying? I know Pearl and Marco are ready to leave. I also have a list of a few of our people ready to go home."

After taking a deep breath, Viera sighed. "I missed the smell of home. We're going to visit my parents for a couple of days, let them meet the kiddo, then we'll all head home."

Once the shock of the baby wore off, and Betsy handed her over, she went over to hug the older children. "Goodness Scout, you're huge!" He looked nearly eleven. "And Tiffany, you could almost legally drive in the U.S."

They both laughed.

Scout spun. "I've missed this planet, though I love being home. I can't wait to meet my new grandparents. What about you Tiffany?"

"Of course not. I think being spoiled will be amazing. And I love swimming in these oceans."

Betsy wasn't sure what had happened to Tiffany's parents, but thought this was a much better arrangement for her.

The group toured the school, Marco and Pearl explaining the theory behind the classes and how they ran everything.

Viera nodded. "So, the students come for lessons and then go home. It's like online, but not, where they can drop in for lessons and labs?"

Pearl nodded as she spoke. "Exactly. There are people who want to master their proficiencies more quickly and they move into one of the small homes we've built on the property. That said, most students are happy with their assigned dorm rooms. They use them when they are here late and want to spend the night or need a place for quiet study. But, as I said, mostly the students don't live here full time."

Once Viera, Thorn, and the kids felt they'd seen everything they needed to see, Thorn asked if she could try to imbue a gem.

Viera snorted and lightly punched her shoulder. "Why don't we head to Florida. It should be just before lunch there. We can spend time with my family, then maybe tomorrow we can come and spend the afternoon here without the baby. You know my Mom or aunts will love watching her."

Thorn drooped. "Fine! I guess." Then she leaned down and gave Viera a kiss. "A few hours alone with you ... I can't imagine the trouble we'll get into." She turned to Marco. "If we take a lesson, do *we* get a dorm room?"

A laugh erupted out of Betsy. "Enough, off with you scoundrels. But no leaving the planet without checking in. I have to see my best friend and your kids at least one more time."

She gave each of them another hug before they left for Florida.

Violet slid an arm around her. "So, when are *we* going to have ourselves a baby Angela?"

Thank you for reading!
Galaxy Revisited

Please Leave a review for this book so others know how much you enjoyed reading it.

Find more information on my books on my website

Harlowe Frost has been a teacher at both the high school and college level. Her parents instilled a love of reading from a young age. She grew up in the queer community. Her favorite genre growing up was fantasy and science fiction, that is, until she discovered urban fantasy and paranormal romance. What she never found in those books was the diversity in background, gender identity, and sexuality she saw in the people around her. She decided if she couldn't find that in what she read, then she would write it herself. This started her writing paranormal romance with a LGBTQ+ background.